THE MAN WHO STOPPED THE DUST

Professor Renhard dies accidentally whilst experimenting with a machine that destroys dust. Meanwhile, when Dr. Anderson operates on a young woman, an accidental slip of the surgeon's knife leads to more than her death. The girl's brother, Gaston — Renhard's manservant — festers with revenge and incriminates Anderson, who is eventually judged as certified insane. When he is then incarcerated in an asylum, Gaston's revenge is complete. However — only Dr. Anderson could avert the catastrophic consequences of Renhard's mad experiments . . .

JOHN RUSSELL FEARN

THE MAN WHO STOPPED THE DUST

Complete and Unabridged

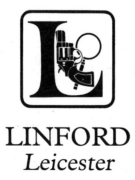

LINFORD
Leicester

First published in Great Britain

First Linford Edition
published 2012

British Library CIP Data

Fearn, John Russell, *1908 – 1960*.
   The man who stopped the dust. - -
(Linford mystery library)
   1. Suspense fiction.
   2. Large type books.
   I. Title II. Series
   823.9′12–dc23

   ISBN 978–1–4448–1293–0

Published by
F. A. Thorpe (Publishing)
Anstey, Leicestershire

Set by Words & Graphics Ltd.
Anstey, Leicestershire
Printed and bound in Great Britain by
T. J. International Ltd., Padstow, Cornwall

This book is printed on acid-free paper

1

The Man Who Stopped the Dust

I

Professor Boris Renhard was a curious, violently temperamental man. A scientist by profession, and something of an idealist by nature, his main objective in life was the improvement of mankind's environment, and the obviation of needless work in order to attain a specified objective. At thirty, he had been a brilliant inventor; at forty he had achieved wealth by that very reason; at fifty his extraordinary power of perception and conception had become a trifle dulled; and at sixty, as we find him now, his great mind was but a ghost of its former self.

It still retained its inventive faculty in some degree, but that careful insight upon cause and effect; that wonderful, almost intuitive sense of being able to see ahead the outcome of almost any invention, was entirely missing.

And that, perhaps, was why he did not foresee the tragic, unbelievable things that were to result from his curious idea of 'stopping the dust.'

He had one confidant, the thirty-five-year-old Dr. Anderson, who did his utmost to keep the professor on the path of sane reasoning — a task of formidable proportions with a temperament so volcanic and didactic as that possessed by Renhard.

It was on a January day of completely unreasonable inclemency when the professor suddenly propounded his latest and most extraordinary theory to his friend.

'Anderson, something has got to be done about all this!' he announced decidedly.

'About what?' Anderson had merely dropped in for one of his weekly chats, which he managed to sandwich between a steadily growing medical practice, and was not feeling particularly intrigued by the possibility of scientific elucidations of the professor's type at the moment. He was standing at the window looking out on the dense London murk.

'About *this!*' Renhard said, jabbing a bony index finger at the pall.

'Oh, you mean the fog? Well, after all, London expects fogs in January — at any time during the winter, in fact. It's had them for centuries. Caused by the evaporation from the Thames, you know.'

'You are telling *me* what causes a fog, John Anderson?' The professor's eyes gleamed. 'Don't I know what *causes* it? What I am going to do is *remedy* it! Science is making great progress in other fields — the bigger, wider fields where my old brain cannot reach; but so mighty are their aims, so celestial their ambitions, they forget the little, everyday inconveniences. They strain at the gnat and swallow the camel, Anderson. I am going to stop a fog, my young friend; more, I am going to stop all dust!'

There was a faint twinkle in the eyes of Anderson. He laid his hand on the elder man's shoulder.

'You get some queer ideas, don't you, professor?'

'There's nothing queer about stopping dust, is there?'

'Nothing except the fact that you can't do it. It's been tried — fog devourers, air-cleaners, molecular vacuums — '

'Fog devourers — bah!' Renhard snorted, and reaching forward snatched up a daily paper from the table. 'Look at that!' he commanded.

' "Four ships lost at sea in the worst fog of years," ' Anderson read aloud. ' "Aircraft lose their way and crash despite radio signals." Well, what about it?' He tossed the paper back onto the table. 'It's one of those things that's inevitable — they call it 'Act of God,' don't they?'

' "Act of God?" ' Renhard groaned and spread his emaciated hands. 'I should have thought that a physician with a rising clientele would have had greater breadth of vision; would have been more ready to admit the possibilities of science. Instead you drivel like a first-grader about the clause of 'Act of God.' A little while ago you hinted at the fact that you knew what a fog is. What exactly *is* the process that causes all this inconvenience and loss

4

of time and life?'

'Why, fog is caused by dust particles, estimated at about 0.001 inch in diameter. The particles might be composed of evaporated ocean spray, disintegrated dust from shooting stars and meteorites, volcanic dust — anything like that. Fog particles are bound to have some kind of dust for their nucleus.'

'Beyond question, we are improving,' said Renhard sourly. 'You admit, freely, that fog is caused by dust particles?'

'Certainly it is. But what of it? You can't stop dust. It is just bound to take place.'

'And as long as it happens life will be endangered,' Renhard added grimly. 'That isn't right, Anderson. Man has brains enough to overcome the difficulty — even as he has overcome everything else.

'You have perhaps heard of the ingenious instrument that contains a pump, a lens, filter papers, and a glass plate divided off into millimetres? Samples of air are sucked into this apparatus, and the number of dust particles determined. In a crowded city there are about 100,000 dust particles to the cubic centimetre; whilst over an ocean the amount is lowered to only 2,000 per cubic centimetre. You appear to know three of the operative factors which cause dust — evaporation of ocean spray, disintegrating shooting stars, volcanic dust; and the fourth is the action of wind over the earth's surface.'

'This sounds more like a treatise on the cause of dust, than how to remedy it,' Anderson remarked dryly.

'If you will be so good as to give me an opportunity, my dear friend, I will come to my point in due time,' Renhard replied acidly.

'Firstly, one must expound the qualities of the particular thing in question, then decide upon the necessary plan to defeat it. We will start again with the phenomenon known as twilight. This happens only because of the refraction of dust particles — the dusty, translucent curtain through which the sun's rays have to pass. Raindrops and hailstones all have a particle of dust within them that serves as the original point upon which to condense. Again, when condensation is sufficiently vigorous, the water vapour becomes small globules of water with the dust speck as the centre — and so clouds are formed.

'Suppose we take an example of how vital a point is volcanic dust. The eruption of the volcano of Krakatoa in or near Java in August, 1883, sent dust twenty miles into the air! That dust impregnated the whole atmospheric envelope and took years to descend. That occurrence provided mankind with some of the most glorious sunrises and sunsets in earthly history. Yet that same beauteous creation can be also the deadliest enemy — the destroyer of life and liberty.'

'Admitted,' Anderson nodded. 'And what do you propose to do next?'

'I am making a machine, Anderson, which will have a 2,000-mile radius of dust elimination when I have completed it. It is what I call a dust vibrator. You admit, of course, that a dust particle is composed of atoms — and that those atoms when aggregated create a molecule?'

'True enough.'

Renhard smiled faintly.

'We are indeed improving. You admit

also that the electron is essential to the structure of an atomic formation — and the atomic formation to the structure of a molecule? Splendid!

'Now, it is conceivable that in time the atoms would lose many of their electrons, owing to the terrific velocity with which the latter move. The disappearance of all electrons would make the weight of the molecule too heavy for the atom to support, and the result would be collapse. That occurrence would take a time that I do not wish to compute, for the simple reason that I evolved a way of destroying all electrons within the molecules that go to make up a dust particle. The result would be collapse of the molecule — and, incidentally, collapse of the dust particle. You get the idea?'

'It certainly sounds all right,' Anderson admitted.

'The electrons can be disrupted — a feat hitherto believed impossible — by vibration. Not an actual force, but a shifting plane of disturbances powerful enough to destroy the electron. The result will be complete absence of dust wherever my vibrator gets to work. Think of that!'

'The idea certainly isn't at all bad,' Anderson said slowly. 'But how exactly do you propose to go about this disruption of the electron? You said something about a vibration — but I'm afraid I'm not so well up in such matters.'

For a space the professor sat in silence. Then:

'I'll make it as clear as I can to your limited understanding, Anderson. I propose to disrupt the electrons by negative electricity in the form of *vibration*. An electron is of course pure negative electricity; it will be repelled by my vibration. Now, electricity, if one gets down to fundamentals, is vibration in a certain form — a vibration of such a periodicity that it becomes light. My vibration will be below that of light. It will be invisible, but tremendously destructive. It will repel and smash an electron completely. In the machine I am making normal electricity is converted into vibration, and when I have finished, the bombardment of electrons will commence — that is, the bombardment of dust electrons.'

'I get all that,' Anderson said, 'but how will you confine your efforts solely to dust? If you disrupt, or rather 'collapse,' the molecules of dust, I don't see what is to prevent the very structure of all matter, since it is all atomic, from collapsing. And that would be catastrophe indeed.'

'There are molecules of different orders,' Renhard answered: 'True, certain things might break down as well as dust — and that is why I am going to project my vibration scheme into the sky, where the only damage that can be done is cloud disruption and dust disruption. That will not affect anything on the earth.'

'Correct me if I'm wrong, professor; but once you have started this disruption, there will be nothing to stop it, will there?'

'Yes. I have evolved the cause of disruption, and the cure,' Renhard answered. 'I have it in my mind what will be necessary to stop the process I create, and thus when I have seen the effects of dust disruption, I will stop the process spreading by setting my subsidiary machine to work. It won't take long to build; anyhow, not long enough for spreading disruption to do much damage.'

Anderson looked uneasy. 'But surely, professor, would it not be better to build your counteracter as well before starting the experiment? To be on the safe side?'

'Needless precaution, Anderson. Besides, I want to be sure that my vibrator works before I go to the expense of building the counteracter. If the machine is a failure, there is no need for me to be too much out of pocket, you know.'

'Something in that,' Anderson confessed. 'If you do succeed in this you will undoubtedly stop the dust, all right.'

'More than that,' Renhard answered slowly. 'I shall be a benefactor of mankind. That is what appeals to me most of all.'

'That all depends on the point of view, of course. Personally, I have always found mankind only too ready to turn on a fellow if his treasured plans don't quite mature to the expectations of the majority.'

Renhard smiled faintly. 'I see, Anderson. You are embittered. Because you once made a slip — because the public held you up as a failure in your work, you have never forgotten.'

'I can never forget that slip of mine.' Anderson brooded through an interval. 'I, a surgeon, on my first great case — a slip of the knife, and a life was lost. I killed a woman with that slip, professor — a young woman. I lost my position as surgeon and became purely a physician. Such things are not easy to forget when — '

'True,' Renhard said; 'but you must learn to forgive and forget whilst you are young enough to do it. Now, may I discuss my plans with you, if you have the time to spare?'

'Why, assuredly. Carry on.'

★   ★   ★

It took Professor Renhard three weeks to purchase and erect his machinery. The erection was accomplished with the aid of Dr. Anderson, when he could spare the time; and upon the night of February 1st, three weeks later, the last bolt had been driven home, and the curious apparatus, a large, complicated mass of machinery, stood before an open window in an empty room at the rear of the professor's luxurious Kensington home.

The view from this window commanded a portion of London's back streets with their glimmering lights; farther beyond were the hazy uprisings of light that betokened the packed and brilliantly illuminated centres of the Strand, Piccadilly Circus, Trafalgar Square, and other nerve centres of the great metropolis.

Dr. Anderson looked up at the frosty, star-studded sky, and then buttoned up his overcoat tightly.

'Everything seems to be in order, Anderson,' Renhard remarked presently. 'I see no reason why we shouldn't experiment.'

Anderson shrugged.

'Just as you like,' he said, coming forward. 'Give her the juice, and we'll see what happens.'

'Right!' Renhard flicked a button on the controlling panel of his vibrator, and it began to purr very softly as the self-acting and self-sustaining generator within proceeded to function.

'It works!' Renhard breathed, rubbing his hands in silent glee.

'I don't see anything,' Anderson said, frowning.

'Nitwit! You don't expect to *see* vibration, do you? The negative electrical energy, being transformed into vibration by the machinery inside here — which after all you know quite as much about as I do, since you helped to assemble it — is even now being hurled forth into the air outside, is invisibly disrupting the atom electrons of dust particles, over an area of two thousand miles. Think of that!'

'I am thinking of it, but I'd like to see something. Listening to this glorified vacuum cleaner of yours isn't exciting enough.'

'Glorified vacuum cleaner!' Renhard exploded. 'You dare make such a comparison?'

Anderson smiled faintly. 'Sorry, prof; I didn't mean to offend you. But look for yourself! The whole thing's a fizzle! Nothing has happened! It certainly does not appear that you'll need to build that counteracter after all.'

The professor moved slowly to the window, taking care to keep out of the direct

14

path of his vibration beam, and looked out on the unchanged view from the window. He bit his lip in vexation.

'Certainly nothing is different there,' he admitted reluctantly. 'I wonder if I made a slip somewhere in my calculations? Let's go to the study and work it out again.'

'All right,' Anderson agreed. 'You'll be catching cold in this ice house if you don't. You always were hopeless at looking after your own comfort. Come on.'

The professor moved disconsolately to his apparatus and reversed the switch upon the panel, which should have put the machine completely out of commission. He was not aware, however, that inside the instrument a whisker of wire had worked loose from the contact screw and was shorting across the two terminals. The movement of the switch only served to cut the machine's power down about fifty per cent; low enough to make its humming imperceptible, but strong enough still to give forth that curious negative vibration to the atoms of dust —

Silently the two passed into the study, and still in silence lighted cigars and sat

15

down. Then the professor brought his fist down on the table with a resounding thump.

'I can't see where there is a mistake,' he growled. 'I worked every bit of the thing out with painstaking care. If there is a fault at all it is either in the apparatus itself, or else we are expecting things to happen too soon. I'll take the infernal thing to bits tomorrow if nothing else presents itself.'

'Well, if that's all there is for it, I may as well be going,' Anderson remarked, rising to his feet. 'I've not had much sleep lately, what with helping you, and trying to get through my own work — '

'I know,' Renhard said, in a quieter tone than usual. 'You've been very good, Anderson, and I appreciate it. I know I'm intolerable at times. I'll have to try to take myself in hand.'

'I should,' Anderson said with a faint smile, pulling his hat down comfortably. 'I — Hm-m-m! Seen my right-hand glove anywhere, prof?'

'Eh? Why, no.'

'I could have sworn I left it on this table with its fellow. Here's one, but where is the other?'

Renhard pressed a button upon his desk, and presently his one manservant, Gaston, appeared.

'You rang, sir?'

'Yes, Gaston. Do you happen to have seen one of Dr. Anderson's gloves about anywhere?'

The peculiar, unaccountably glowing eyes of Gaston turned to Anderson, then back to the professor.

'No, sir, I have seen no trace of the glove in question.'

'Very well, Gaston, thank you.'

Anderson shrugged. 'Well, it doesn't matter. See you tomorrow, prof. Good night.'

'Good night, Anderson.' Renhard answered absently. He sat for a time in deep thought after his friend had gone. Then he arose to his feet and went once again in the direction of the back room where his apparatus was housed.

'Must be the apparatus itself,' he mused, for about the fiftieth time. 'I'll fix it tomorrow, but it occurs to me I had better shut the window and stop this devilish draft whistling down the passages.'

He entered the room, picked his way

among the electric cables and impedimenta, and presently came to the window, reaching up and seizing the frame.

It was as he performed that action that it seemed as though a knife of white-hot steel was passing through his body. He gasped with sudden pain and dropped involuntarily to his knees. It came again, but more piercing and terrific, snapping the life out of his vitals.

He turned his head and saw that he was in a dead line with the vibrator lens. But surely he had switched it off — ? something said in his pain-bemused mind. He made a last gasping effort to call for help, to call Gaston; then a sledgehammer blow seemed to rip his brain asunder. He collapsed without another sound to the floor, stone dead, his vibrator still issuing forth its mysterious negative energy —

II

Dr. Anderson awoke early the following morning with the distinct inner conviction that somewhere something was amiss. What it was he could not define. It was a very acute form of that peculiar sense of coming danger that we all feel at times in everyday life.

It was still dark when he awoke; and a glance at his luminous watch showed him it was six thirty. The room was in darkness, and the only sound was the deep breathing of his wife.

Following his usual custom after his ablutions, he crossed to the window to open it and allow the fresh morning air to enter, so that he could perform his brief breathing exercises. Humming a ditty to himself in a pleasing baritone, he slipped back the catch and flung the frosted glass sash wide open. It faced the east, and it was just past the hour of sunrise.

At what he beheld, poor Anderson nearly fainted and dropped through the window. Not quite doing this, he collapsed limply upon the window frame, supported by his forearms, and stared with goggling eyes to the east, muttering soundless words.

The sun was in the sky, just clear of the horizon — but what in Heaven's name had happened to it? It was just a blazing, yellow-white ball, with a vague hint of solar prominences caressing its edges, rising in an almost dead black sky! The stars were still shining, despite the sunlight. Nature was suddenly intoxicated.

'Great God!' Anderson whispered at last, drawing himself up and trying to imagine if there was perhaps some kind of eclipse in progress.

'No — no eclipse,' he said to the dawn. 'It's something else!'

Recovering from his first terrific shock, he tightened the girdle round his gown, and marched off downstairs — to encounter Cawley, his manservant. For once in his imperturbable life, Cawley was looking oddly shaken and uncertain. He jumped as Anderson almost violently clutched his arm.

'Cawley — I'm not mad, am I?' Anderson asked quickly.

'If you refer to the dawn, sir, no. You are quite sane — but, with all respect, sir, it's a hell of a queer thing!'

'I'll forgive your language, Cawley. It's

apt, for once.' Anderson stood still and thought for a moment, then he glanced again at his watch. 'Cawley, I do believe I have an idea what is causing all this! The professor! Renhard! The vibrator! Of course! What an idiot I am!'

'Beg pardon, sir?' Cawley elongated himself into stiff servility.

'Nothing, Cawley, nothing at all. Just thinking aloud. Listen carefully. I'm going out. When Mrs. Anderson comes down, tell her I'll return shortly; tell her that I've been called away on a very urgent case. Urgent! I'll say it is! The most urgent I've ever known. You understand, Cawley?'

'Perfectly, sir.'

Within ten minutes, Anderson was dressed, and stepped out into that astounding dawn. Almost immediately he became aware of pale, frightened faces staring up at the inky skies, of milk boys and news vendors shouting with a tremor in their usually husky voices, of frightened glances cast to all points of the compass, as though in expectation of some approaching terror. Anderson reflected that he was perhaps the only man in

London who could smile under the circumstances. Of course, that infernal vibrator had worked — but too effectively!

Another thing Anderson noticed as he plodded on to the professor's home was the utter blackness of shadows when out of the sunlight. They were like ink, triangular enigmas in which he floundered about helplessly, able to see the sun beyond, yet not a thing where he stood. Diffusion of light, refraction, had gone.

He was bruised, hot and troubled when he finally arrived at the professor's home, only to be met by another shock. Two policemen were at the gate, and a little knot of curious sightseers were gazing at the closed front door. Even the astounding sky failed to impress them, evidently.

As Anderson made to turn in at the gateway, a strong, blue-clothed arm detained him.

'Sorry, sir, you can't go in there.'

Anderson looked blankly at the constable. He seemed very solid and unworried.

'Can't go in? Why not?'

'There's been a murder. Professor Renhard, who used to own this house, has been killed.'

'Killed!' Anderson clutched the gate-post for support. 'But — but that's quite impossible! Why, I was only talking to him last night! I'm his greatest friend — Dr. Anderson. I *must* go in, I tell you!'

It seemed that a strange light entered the constable's eyes.

'Dr Anderson, eh? That's different, then. You'd better come in and see Inspector Wade.'

Anderson was escorted into the famil-iar study, and there beheld another constable and a plainclothes man. This latter personage looked Anderson up and down sharply.

'You are a friend of Professor Renhard's?'

'I am his greatest friend, his dearest confidant. My name is Anderson.'

'You can prove that?'

'Of course. Gaston, the servant, will do that. Ring for him.'

The inspector complied, and presently Gaston was before them.

'This gentleman here says his name is Anderson and that he is a close friend of Professor Renhard's. Or rather he was. Is that so?'

Gaston's strange eyes were gleaming.

'Yes, sir, that is Anderson, certainly.' Then he turned aside and muttered something in the inspector's ear. The inspector nodded grimly.

'Dr. Anderson, when did you last see Professor Renhard alive?'

'Last night. He was in perfect health. Where was he found? How do you know he was murdered?'

'He was found in the room next door here — with a knife hilt deep in his heart!'

'A knife!' Anderson echoed in horror. 'But — but — '

'A surgical knife; I believe it's called a scalpel,' the inspector proceeded in a slow, grim voice. 'And what is even more peculiar, it bears your name on the hilt!'

'My name! But there is some absurd mistake here, inspector — '

'I don't think so,' returned the implacable voice. 'I was intending to have you looked up in any case, but it seems there is some truth in the old adage that a criminal always returns to the scene of the crime!'

Anderson straightened up. His face was suddenly crimson with sheer indignation.

'What the devil are you talking about?'

The inspector did not answer. Instead he led the way into the adjoining room. Mute, Anderson looked about him. The professor's body lay where it had fallen by the open window. The only other peculiarities were that the vibrator had ceased to function completely — not that Anderson considered there was anything unusual in this, since he fully believed it had been switched off properly the night before — and that a surgical knife was buried in the professor's chest, directly above the heart. A crimson stain discoloured his coat and the white boards of the floor.

In silence Anderson went down on one knee and looked at the knife closely without touching it. Sure enough, his name was neatly executed on the ivory hilt.

'Why, this knife vanished from my surgical instruments years ago, just a few days after I had performed an unsuccessful operation on a woman,' he said, looking up, startled. 'How in the name of the devil did it get there?'

'That is a question only you can answer,' Inspector Wade replied coldly. 'I will reconstruct your crime. First, you entered here last night by some means or other, got the professor into this room, and killed him with this queer machine, which in some diabolical way broke every bone in the professor's body — even his skull! I have that fact from experiments on his dog — you see its body over there. We switched on that damnable contrivance and found that it destroys life. Lastly, to make sure of your victim you stabbed him to the heart with a surgical knife. Your motive is at present unknown. Then you departed, but, unfortunately, you left your glove behind on the floor here.'

'A glove?' Anderson turned startled eyes to his own right-hand glove lying on the floor. Vainly his mind tried to link things together. 'But I lost that last evening, and asked Gaston if he had seen it, when the professor was *alive*!'

'Gaston saw you return and commit the deed!' said the toneless voice.

'Gaston saw me return!' Anderson repeated incredulously. 'But — but the man's crazy! I never killed the professor with this machine! It's an instrument for taking the dust out of the air, and that is what has caused this black sky this morning. It splits electrons and — '

'You dare to make use of a perfectly natural eclipse to aid your tissue of lies?' the inspector thundered.

'Eclipse! But this isn't an eclipse. In that case the sun would be obliterated, and there would be distinct evidences of the corona!'

'I'm scientist enough without your explanations,' the inspector snapped; then, turning to the constable behind him: 'All right, take him away. He'll have to be medically examined. There's neither sense nor reason in this butchery. Out with him.'

Utterly dazed and dumbfounded, the

unfortunate Anderson was whirled into the next room and handcuffed for a moment to the massive iron fireplace while the constable departed to call a car. As he stood there, panting and furious, Anderson became aware of the sleek, strange-eyed Gaston standing beside him. He was smiling bitterly.

'Well?' Anderson snapped venomously. 'What in hell are you laughing at, you swine?'

'Remember the young woman you killed in that operation, Anderson? Remember the young girl, aged just twenty-four — young and beautiful and charming — suffering from a mere abdominal growth that any surgeon should have removed without difficulty? And remember how your knife slipped? How you killed her? Destroyed her?'

Gaston's lips writhed back from strong teeth in a deadly snarl. 'That girl was my sister, you devil! My sister, all in the world to me, and I entrusted her to the hands of a — a *butcher!* But the knife that killed her will kill you! I stole it from your instruments; yes, I've kept it all these years, and waited and waited for the moment when I could get you where I wanted you. You will be certified mad, Anderson; I will see to that! I know enough about the vibrator to stop and start it, and I'm hoping to experiment to the full while you are in a cell — a padded one, I hope! Yes, I took your glove. I stabbed Renhard after he had died through getting in the way of the vibrator after it was supposedly switched off, and actually was not, because of a loose whisker of wire.'

'I did not purposely kill your sister, you fool!' Anderson panted. 'It was a mistake; too much talc powder in my glove — my hand slipped on the knife. I have never operated since.'

'No, and you never will again,' Gaston muttered. 'I'll see to that, Butcher Anderson!'

* * *

The law was ruthless with the unfortunate, helpless Anderson. Before he scarcely realized what had happened, and mainly owing to the insidious tongue of the vengeful witness, Gaston, he was certified insane, inclined to violence with murderous intent, and promptly removed to an asylum. All the efforts of his distracted wife and influential friends failed completely to alter the decision.

He was probably the only man at that time who could possibly hope to avert the catastrophe that only too plainly was approaching from this mad idea of stopping the dust.

III

And things began to happen in the outside world. In some ways, Gaston was a scientific man. He understood what the vibrator did — that it destroyed dust, and human life also, if one chanced to get in direct line with the stream of vibration. So it came about that Gaston operated the machine to his own satisfaction, pointing it always to the black sky, until one day an accident happened.

Somewhere inside the instrument a

wire or piece of mechanism slipped, and all the external efforts of Gaston failed completely to stop the machine running. The interior he dared not explore for fear of coming into contact with the deadly energy. He feared that stored-up energies might be released if he investigated too closely.

Thus the machine just ran on, he himself becoming more afraid of it every day, striving to think of a way around the difficulty, but failing. Only Anderson knew enough about the machine to stop it and repair it — and he was safely put away. Gaston from then on became a peculiar study in hatred and fear.

On the day of Anderson's arrest, London experienced the most amazing morning of its life — a morning that brought about an almost incredible return of religious revivalists and so-called seers, who read in the black, sun-and-starlit sky, a potent message of impending destruction from the Almighty.

Collisions in the streets were remarkably frequent, occasioned mainly by the absolute blackness of the shadows of buildings. In these shadows it was as black as Erebus; there was no diffusion of light whatever, and the result was that, in areas greatly overhung by tall buildings, buses and motor cars crashed helplessly into each other, drivers strangely confused by the swirling lights of approaching traffic, and unable to distinguish the innocent from the dangerous. Even collisions between pedestrians were equally prevalent, and the hospitals experienced the busiest morning for years, treating casualties.

Toward noon, as the black sky and panic continued unabated, a deputation visited Greenwich Observatory. The official in charge was sympathetic, but vague. He confessed that he had no idea what had caused the celestial phenomenon. The only explanation possible was that by some peculiar means all the processes of refraction and de-fraction had suddenly become set at naught — perhaps through an agency of some annihilating gas in outer space, through which the earth, following her orbit, was passing.

It was not a cheering observation, at the best.

Naturally, the reporters of the leading newspapers were quick to turn the information to their own uses, flavoured, as ever, by their own distinctive 'scare' methods. The first evening newspaper editions were permitted to have bolder, larger headlines than usual.

EARTH IN DANGER OF DESTRUCTION! DISTURBANCES IN OUTER SPACE THREATEN THE EARTH!

The man in the street, to whom the newspaper is all-in-all, the peak of perfect information, became a trifle worried. Business became jerky. In subways, trains and buses, the one topic of conversation was the black sky. Men and women who, previously had been so absorbed with their daily task that they would have been surprised at being told the sky's normal colour was blue, suddenly took on astronomical tendencies and revealed latent and unsuspected scientific qualities.

Cinema audiences, and audiences at all

public halls, were curiously restive that night. The condition lasted at the cinema until the show began, then at what they beheld the audience sat in sudden awed silence, astonished at what they saw.

For the screen images were cut as though with stencil — were almost three dimensional! Yet between the screen and the projector box there was no *beam*.

The more thoughtful of the audience pondered over this curious fact. More than one puzzled operator surveyed the screen with troubled eyes, unable to account for the sudden blinding brilliance, which certainly had not been in evidence the day before. Other operators studiously checked their mechanisms — and found everything in order. The trouble, whatever it was, must be in the air itself. And another occurrence in the cinema theatre upon which almost everybody remarked was the almost unnatural clearness of the sound apparatus. Every word was clear-cut and keen; the most mumbling actor could be heard distinctly, and those who were acknowledged masters of elocution seemed as though they were going to walk right out of the screen and come down into the audience, so lifelike was the effect.

Outside, the astounding clearness of sound was again evidenced. The very air seemed to crackle with crispness. The hooting of tugs on the Thames came clear and shrill above the deeper roaring note of the traffic.

It was a suddenly changed world — a world of unaccountable happenings, a world in which sound and actual light had increased, and yet where silence and darkness were more profound than ever before.

And still, in a little laboratory in Kensington, reposed the answer to the riddle.

By midnight London, for a change, was comparatively silent. The populace, worried by the events of the extraordinary day, had retired earlier than usual. Hundreds heard Big Ben chime that night who had never heard it before, so distinctly did the sound carry through the still air.

The following morning, the sky was still black; once more there was an unearthly sunrise of a blazing yellow-white ball that shed its pitiless brilliance on a panicky city. Then it became known that this black area had only a radius of two thousand miles, and beyond that radius was the blue sky and sunshine and shadows which man holds dear. As a result an exodus to places beyond the two-thousand-mile limit began.

The newspapers, as usual, were full of remarkable information, the most important being two columns by the astronomical correspondent upon the finding, by the observers of Greenwich Observatory, of several new galaxies that had never been seen before! Also observations of Mars and Venus were greatly simplified, the markings on their respective surfaces being startlingly clear and comparatively free from vibration.

It did actually jar the ordinary businessman to discover that, despite a night of intense coldness, there was no trace of frost the following morning. Nor dew! Yet the air was keen — incredibly, strangely keen.

There was one man, however, who

surveyed the strange happenings from a scientific angle.

His name was not prepossessing — Samuel Brown — and his personality was obscure. To the outer world, Sam Brown was a lawyer's clerk, but there were some who knew him to be a man of natural scientific talents, who now found ample scope for his hobby in the sudden odd happenings that had come to pass.

It was on the second evening that he confided his opinions to his not-too-brilliant wife.

'Elsie, there's something more behind all this business than an agency in outer space!'

His wife sewed deliberately for a space, then cocked one doubtful and slightly protruding blue eye upon him.

'Suppose there is? What are you going to do about it, Sam?'

'I don't know — yet, but I'm going to have a shot at doing something. The death roll is mounting day by day. This is the time for those who understand a little to expound their views! The scientists are baffled, but I'm not so sure that I am.'

He screwed his head round, struck by a sudden thought, and pensively surveyed the sideboard — a massive heirloom from his great-grandmother. Then he ducked his head, and looked intently along the top of the thing.

'If you're looking for dust, Sam, you'll find plenty!' his wife remarked presently. 'I haven't cleaned that sideboard for days. What with cooking and washing, I never get the time. Why you don't get a smaller sideboard instead of that lumbering thing, I don't know.'

Sam looked up, pondered for a moment, then quietly but forcibly took his wife's arm and led her, protesting feebly, across the room. When they came to the sideboard he pushed her head down with delightful familiarity until her eyes were level with the sideboard top.

'Look along there!' he commanded.

She obeyed, and then gave a sharp exclamation.

'Why, Sam, you've cleaned it for me! Why — and the polished wood round the carpet edge, too! What's come over you?'

Sam slowly shook his head. 'No, Elsie, I

haven't cleaned anything. The solution is exactly what I've believed all along. *There is no dust!*'

And he stood looking at her solemnly, his round face full of the intensity of his statement.

Elsie's brows knitted. 'No dust, Sam? Oh, go on with you!'

'I mean it, Elsie. Here — come to the table and I'll figure it out for you.'

They sat down. Sam tore the margin from the evening paper and produced a stump of pencil; then he proceeded to execute what he was pleased to call 'higher mathematics'.

'Totally black sky, amazingly brilliant lights, remarkable astronomical observations, inky shadows, clear sound, and now — no dust on a polished surface. Elsie, somebody or something is annihilating dust!'

'You — you mean stopping it, Sam?'

'Yes, stopping it. But why, and how, is the point. I'm going to sort this out.'

Elsie sighed and thoughtfully scratched the end of her nose. 'And we've only just bought a new vacuum cleaner! If there's no dust, we shan't need it.'

Sam smiled grimly. 'Elsie, there'll be a lot of things we shan't need if this dustless world goes on. But it won't go on! I promise you that!'

His wife resumed her armchair and sniffed.

IV

'Gentlemen,' said the chairman of the Cleenwurld Vacuum Company's board of directors, 'our sales have dropped nearly seventy-five per cent during the past week. It is a week since this strange condition of a dustless, rainless, dayless world began. And our firm is on the brink of disaster! These conditions cannot go on!'

Unfortunately, however, the chairman found no means of preventing the conditions from going on, with the result that shortly afterward, in common with other dust-removing devices, the Cleenwurld Vacuum Company vanished from the commercial map.

About the same time, the street-cleaners of London were summoned and at once instructed to cease work. London was a city without dust. One or two mechanical contrivances could quite easily cope with paper litter and other details. So it was in every case where dust was the fundamental of employment. The figures of unemployment began to mount.

Little by little the grey face of London underwent a change as the eighth day of black sky and blazing sun appeared. The buildings, buried for years in the grime and filth of ages, began to reveal their real faces from under the canopy. The dust was disappearing from their black façades and soot-encrusted ornamentations. Here and there the long-hidden eyes of gargoyles appeared and looked out anew on the infinite strangeness of the dustless city. The grey dinginess of the Thames Embankment took on a clean newness, as though sprayed with some all-powerful cleansing fluid.

Everywhere dust was on the march, was vanishing and exploding beneath the force of the still-unchecked vibrator in the centre of the city. The exploding of the dust atoms that had begun in the upper reaches of the air had now spread downward to the lower quarters — was making itself manifest in every nook and cranny.

Limehouse, long lost in the filth and dirt of accumulated centuries, became a place of slowly whitening wonder. At each turn one was met by a building or street rendered suddenly and unaccountably unfamiliar by the change in its appearance. Even the grime of the great railway stations began to vanish, and as time passed Londoners were presented with the incredible spectacle of seeing Euston and other stations rearing up as bright-red buildings with clean glass roofs, every engraved foundation stone as clear-cut and plain to read as though an army of cleaners had scrubbed at them for centuries.

So complex is the human mind, so unexpected man's reaction to environment, it was considered quite natural when the earlier fears of the populace changed into awe and then pride. They became accustomed to the black sky, and powerful floodlighting now rendered shadows no longer dangerous. The first disasters were now absent. The travel companies, ever up to the topic of the moment, advertised cheap fares for visitors from other lands to come to view the transformation of a city.

So it was at first. Then, presently, rather alarming reports began to be received by the world's press.

The blackness was spreading!

It covered an area now of three thousand miles, and was spreading gradually with every hour, in a fan shape. The annihilation of dust atoms would go on, now it was started, until something was found to counteract it. Dr. Anderson, in his asylum cell, heard this news indirectly, and cursed the fates, circumstances, and Gaston.

With this new information, fear began to reappear slowly — the novelty died away. The benefit of disappearing dust and its consequent lightening of labour, the rising of new clean cities out of the black masks of the old, could not allay that new deep-rooted fear. The terrible thought that perhaps blue sky would never return began to become an obsession. The fear heightened when a strange illness broke out in London. It commenced with a sensation of irritation upon the skin, more particularly on exposed parts, which rapidly spread to the entire body, finally to the mouth, and then caused death from uncontrollable coughing.

The physicians could not understand the malady in the least; it was something that had never been known before. They were still in the dark when there appeared none other than Samuel Brown himself, neat, inconspicuous, and carrying a brief case in his hand. After a great deal of trouble he was admitted to the sanctum of the head surgeon of the most important institution — Dr. Long.

Dr. Long was not very gracious.

'It is to be hoped, Mr. Brown,' said this individual testily, 'that you have something of import to convey. Only on those conditions can I possibly spare the time to converse with you.'

44

Brown smiled slightly. 'You may perhaps feel a trifle more disposed to converse when you are aware that I have come to tell you what is the cause of the peculiar malady that has broken out in the dark areas.'

Dr. Long permitted himself a faintly cynical smile.

'You are the fourth person today who has undertaken to explain that,' he said coldly.

'Man is ever ready to make capital out of either accident or circumstance,' Brown responded calmly. 'I know what I am talking about. I have not come here to waste your time. As a lawyer's clerk I know that time is valuable, and — '

'A lawyer's clerk! And you dare to come here and attempt to expound the nature of a new disease! Sir, this is preposterous!'

'But the truth, all the same. Dr. Long, the cause of this deadly disease is dust destruction!'

'Dust destruction?' Dr. Long's eyebrows shot up and then down again. He fixed the unmoved Sam with a deadly stare.

'The cause of the black skies and a

45

clean London is occasioned by the same thing — annihilation of dust,' Sam went on steadily. 'The trouble has now spread to human beings, who are always, no matter how clean, covered with a certain amount of dust. This dust is disrupting upon their skin, and, when it reaches the mouth and nose, sets up a fatal irritation. That is the explanation.'

'Utter rubbish!' Dr. Long snapped hotly. 'I have never heard such balderdash in the course of my entire professional career. The disease is simply an advanced form of — er — erysipelas.'

'You do well to hesitate before using that word,' Sam said grimly. 'You know as well as I do, Dr. Long, that this disease is as much apart from erysipelas as the North Pole is from the South. You don't like being taught your job; that's what's the matter with you!'

'How dare you, sir? How dare you? I am sorry, Mr. Brown, but I have no time for you. Good day!' The strong chin projected adamantly.

Sam shrugged. 'Very well, then, Dr. Long. But you will be *very* sorry you have no time for me. Good day to you.'

From there Sam went direct to his flat. His wife, curiously greasy and besmudged, with a cretonne apron tied almost painfully round her middle, came shuffling into the little drawing room as he entered.

'What's the matter, Sam? Why aren't you at the office?'

'Because I've more important things to do, Elsie. Law doesn't interest me when the fate of a planet is at stake. Here I am, with the one cure for a world disease in my very hands — written down on these very papers — and Dr. Long won't listen to me because it looks as though I'm telling him his own job. Bah! The little-mindedness of it all! I think I prejudiced him by telling him I was a lawyer's clerk. Had I given the Russian name of 'Brownofski,' and presented myself with a bushy beard and a fierce compulsion in my eyes, I might have got somewhere with him.'

'Well, I told you to stick to law, Sam.' Elsie wiped her lard-smeared hands on her apron and thoughtfully sucked a hollow back tooth. 'You should have stuck to your affidavits and — '

'Elsie,' Sam interrupted her suddenly, 'I married you because I loved you — and I still do — but if you keep on harping on what I ought to have done, instead of what I am going to do, I'll hit you over your dense head with your own rolling pin! So think that over. Now get on with your cooking, and leave me to think.'

'Oh, all right — but goodness knows what you're going to think with.'

'Something you haven't got, if you must know!' Sam snapped. 'Now clear out!'

Elsie slowly obeyed, and Sam did set himself to think — hard. He spent a time gazing out of the window over the lowering roofs of the tenement houses contiguous to his own flat. Then he looked up at the black sky.

'Either a devil or a saint,' he whispered. 'Either the creator of this trouble sought to improve the world, or else he sought to make it a world of terror. The destruction of dust! Now what could cause that? Vacuum? Not on such a scale. Or tremendous wind pressure? No; that would necessitate a gale, and it has been as still as the grave ever since this business started. Electricity? Hm-m-m — that might be responsible for anything, as so little is really known of its fundamentals. I'll work that out.'

After some difficulty he located a writing pad and flung it on the table beneath the electric light — a light that had never been extinguished for nine days except during sleep, for the flat was in the shadow — and set to work to figure the matter out. The moment he began, Sam Brown, the clerk, vanished, and the precise, unerring mind of the true scientist came into being.

By the time Elsie had shuffled in again he had the thing clear in his mind.

'Elsie,' he said decisively, it's disruption. Electrical disruption. Figures prove that it could be done.'

'What's electrical dis- dis — -whatever you called it?' Elsie inquired.

'Disruption of the atoms, of the molecules, of the very *being* of dust, by some electrical energy.'

'Well, now you've found that out, what do you propose doing about it?'

'I'm going to *stop* it!'

49

'How?'

'By an improved system of my cure for the disease.' He paused, marshalling his thoughts.

'You see, when the atoms of dust start to disrupt upon a human being, the only thing to stop it is the removal of the dust atoms themselves. I didn't know until I worked it out that it was the *atoms* of dust that were causing the trouble. I merely thought the dust itself was somehow disrupting. The thing to stop the latter condition would be a very powerful but minute electrical vacuum capable of drawing off every particle of dust from a human form. That would stop the disruption spreading until it became fatal. Once it reaches the vital organs nothing can be done about it, of course; the thing to do is to check it in its incipiency.

'But now that I know it is the atoms of dust that are being disrupted — possibly the disintegration of the electrons causing collapse of the atomic structure — I can work even more successfully. The dust atoms that are whole must be *divided* from the disrupting atom areas by a beam or shield of sufficient vibration to prevent the further disruption of atoms continuing. Like an asbestos screen would stop a fire spreading any further. You get the idea? A shield *between* the disrupting sections and the whole sections. And it must be vibration capable of exerting a negative effect upon the exploding atoms. That will require some working out.'

'And you gave up a steady job to discover that!' Elsie sighed. 'I've not the least idea what you're talking about, and I'm not altogether sure that you have, either.'

Sam chuckled. 'Leave it to me, Elsie. You won't regret this day. You'll rejoice in the future that it ever came to be. Now be a good girl and leave me to work in peace.'

V

The next two days brought trouble and strife in the dustless world. The farmers rose in a body and made a vehement deputation to the government — an urge to make some attempt to remove the conditions that were existing. Plants and crops were commencing to die from the continued lack of moisture. Never a cloud was seen in the sky — it remained coal-black; never any dew or frost. All rivers and brooks were at the lowest ebb for years, and becoming still less.

And now a greater and more serious problem was hovering on the landscape. Water was coming to an end! The chief water office engineers for London and environs reported that the water supply in the reservoirs was dropping lower and lower, and there was not the vaguest chance of rain. Little by little troubled humanity began to realize that it was being forced into a tight corner.

The water shortage was the seed of disaster creeping over the world with the gradual spreading of the dark areas. More and more remote was becoming the view of a blue sky. Sam Brown, realizing this, worked night and day, that he might have a blue, dusty portion of sky left on which to experiment.

The advance of time brought about

water rations. Public transport services were curtailed. Even automobiles were run only occasionally, for the water ration made it almost prohibitive to use water in the radiators. For a time milk and spirits were used, but after a while, with the slow dying of cattle, even this ceased.

So desperate was the position becoming, a conference of the world's governments was convened to review the situation. It was at best a pretty absurd idea, with the cancer now so far advanced, but public force demanded action.

The meeting, naturally, came to nothing. Nobody could explain the cause of the trouble and nobody knew how to stop it. The idea of consulting some of the great scientists and electricians never seemed to occur to these political geniuses. Probably the idea was as far from their minds as the thought of Sam Brown having the key to the problem in his hands.

For he most undoubtedly had.

So, very gradually, utter and complete catastrophe began to make itself felt. In all countries where the dark areas were at their worst, trouble was rife. Death, famine, and pestilence were the order. Cattle, plants, trees, the very grass was shrivelling, warped and withered under the black, star-and-sun-ridden sky. At night there was no change, save for the fact that the sun vanished to give place to a steely moon, and strange, hitherto unknown constellations gleamed forth from various quarters of the heavens.

Presently, efforts were made to filter the oceans, but so complicated was the task, and so short the water to give to the workers, that the idea fizzled out. To supply the world with filtered seawater became a stillborn idea on the threshold of impending death.

London, New York, Berlin, Paris, Brussels, Vienna — all were no longer cities of business. They were cities of thirst and misery, of pestilence and incurable disease. And yet everything, by grim irony, was as bright and clean as though washed with flowing streams. Nowhere a speck of dust — and nowhere a drop of water!

Only a track of five hundred miles of blue sky now remained, and this had its centre over the plains of Central Russia — the one point in the world where the atomic disruption had not yet reached, where the consummation of dust destruction still hung fire.

But, minute by minute that stretch was narrowing; minute by minute, the sky of man was melting away.

★ ★ ★

It was at this point in the tragic history of stopping dust that Sam Brown completed his invention. It was a brilliant piece of work, but only his eyes admitted the fact. To his wife it was a cumbersome affair of boxes and dials that consumed a great deal of privately generated electricity to keep it going — for the ordinary current had long since ceased, owing to failure of water energy.

'My figures prove that it works, Elsie,' Sam said. 'The only way I can get help is by getting somebody to finance me to Central Russia where the remaining path of blue sky exists. If that gap vanishes, I'm powerless! All dust will be gone and I can't separate the normal from the explosive. I'm going to the government — to Downing Street — right away.'

'Downing Street?' his wife echoed.

'Yes, and if I don't come back, don't worry. I haven't a moment to lose: I'll return when my work is ended. Now be a good sort and help me pack these things up.'

At Downing Street, Sam was listened to attentively, mainly because of his earnestness, his apparatus, and his perfectly logical reasoning. The chairman of the meeting, at Sam's request, sent for an electrical expert from Greenwich, and this individual, after checking up Brown's figures, sat in awed silence for a while.

'Mr. Brown, it's a masterpiece!' he declared at last. 'If the cause of the disruption is what you think it is, then undoubtedly this machine will stop it, I — ' He paused, and the chairman frowned as a clerk entered, bearing a card.

'All right,' the chairman growled. 'Show him in, please.'

A tall man with bushy eyebrows entered — and bowed stiffly.

'Your mission is urgent, Dr. Long?' the chairman asked. 'I am much occupied.'

'My mission is a matter of life and death. People are dying by hundreds. It is essential that something be done. Everybody must help in this crisis. I wish you to have the government issue an order that all houses are to be opened up for public service — as hospitals. I seek your most earnest cooperation, and — '

Dr. Long paused and stared hard at Sam, who had just raised his face from his notes.

'Mr. Brown!' he exclaimed. 'You!'

'Who else?' Sam inquired pleasantly. 'But don't let me interrupt you, doctor.'

'I've been searching all over London for you,' Long said intensely, clutching the unmoved Sam's arm. 'You never left your address when you visited me. That cure of yours! We are ready to try it! Ready to do anything to try to stop this malady — '

Sam shrugged. 'I have had too much important business elsewhere recently to try and interest other dolts in my antidote for the malady,' he remarked coldly. 'Here are the papers — take them and perhaps they'll help you to learn that nobody is ever too clever to learn.'

Long almost snatched the papers and raced from the room.

'Mr. Brown,' the chairman remarked, 'it indeed seems as though you are going to be our saviour. We will do anything you wish; even if you do not succeed it cannot make things any worse. What are your orders?'

'The fastest possible airplane to Central Russia. I require several trained electric experts, and a good pilot who knows his way to the one remaining fragment of blue sky by the shortest route. That is all.'

'It shall be done immediately, Mr. Brown.'

★　　★　　★

So it came about that when the last stretch of blue sky in the entire world had shrunk to only ten miles in width, Sam Brown set up his apparatus among the barren hills and plains of Central Russia, amid cutting winds and bitter cold, surrounded by his little group of picked experts, two high-powered aircraft, and

the intensely anxious government representative.

'If my theories are correct, the vibration
energy from this instrument of mine
should give a fan-shaped extension of
vibration upward to a fourteen-mile
limit,' Brown said: 'If we calculate the
velocity of the disrupting vibration at 180
frequencies — and that is about what I
think it is — it stands to reason that the
frequency of my 'curtain,' working trans-
verse to the disrupting energy, and having
a frequency of over 2,000, will block the
path of the disrupting atoms and save that
bit of normal sky which is left. After that,
when the last of the disrupting atoms on
the disruptive side of my screen have
exploded, we can remove the shield, and
very gradually the dust will again spread
and multiply from that blueness, and
disseminate throughout the world again.
We will build fires, make great smoke
columns, do hundreds of things to make
dust.

'Now, are we ready?'

The instruments were set up in their
predetermined positions, and for a time

everything was strain and anxiety. Sam flitted about in his huge overcoat like some goblin, peering at this and inspecting that until at last he raised his hand and gave the signal.

Sam Brown's apparatus immediately worked, and a pinkish screen spread outward and upward toward the blue sky that remained, its edges sharply notched out with the encroaching black.

In utter silence the watchers stared upward; then with a bitter oath Sam tore off his hat and flung it on the iron-hard ground.

'Failed!' he groaned hoarsely. 'Look! The black is still spreading! My judgment has been at fault.'

'But your figures — your calculations!' the electrical expert protested.

'I know that, but — '

Brown stopped dead; then suddenly he snapped his fingers.

'Got it! Whatever is causing the disruption is still working, and it is stronger than my apparatus. I underestimated its power.'

He looked round on his silent colleagues.

'Gentlemen, we have about twenty-four

hours in which to locate the instrument that is causing the damage, and get back here. What are we to do?'

The engineers scratched their heads, the government representative stroked his chin, and two plane pilots fingered their coat belts. And above the blackness encroached a trifle further through the pink screen.

'We have not the time,' the government expert said at last. 'We have not the time.'

Back in London, however, certain curious events were taking place.

At the house of the late Professor Renhard, a wild-eyed, unshaven individual was creeping down the stairs in utter silence. He crept down the hall and opened the front door. Then, like some hunted animal, he descended to the street — a street lit by the sun in the black sky; a street devoid of traffic, where the corpses of dogs and cats lay scattered here and there.

'Destruction! Death!' Gaston murmured. 'Because I couldn't stop the machine! I cannot stand it any longer. I must find Anderson! Do you hear, *I must find Anderson*!' he shouted to the black, starry skies, and wandered through the inky shadows, only one thought in his burning brain, tottering on the brink of insanity through lack of water, and a nursed revenge.

Tattered and unkempt, he drifted through the streets, halting ever and again at a despairing shout, slinking into the pitchy darkness as a huddled form would slink past him like an animal in the gloom.

Fear, darkness, and death. The three grim ghouls stalked through all the cities of the world.

At the gates of the asylum where he knew Anderson was imprisoned, Gaston collapsed. He was carried inside by attendants, into the main office.

'Anderson!' he muttered, clutching the coat lapel of the supervising officer. 'I must see him! Let him free! *Set him free*! He is not mad; he is the only man who really knows how to stop this world disaster — how to take away this black sky. I got him in here by a trick. For God's sake, let him out!'

'We can't take your word for it,' said the officer stolidly. 'There are many formalities to be gone through.'

Gaston sat up and looked at the officials with burning eyes. Then suddenly he whipped out a loaded revolver from his hip pocket. 'Will you do as I say or not?' he demanded thickly. 'Hurry, you idiots! There'll be no red tape this time — just action!'

Other officials appeared, but they hesitated at the vision of Gaston's blazing eyes and the revolver. Holding them at bay; dodging about with superhuman agility, he circumvented their every move, until at last he had forced them into the main corridor of cells.

'Get busy!' he commanded; and the wardens, all weakened by the strain of recent events, and their own torturing thirst, obeyed — obeyed with a weakness which certainly would never have obtained under normal circumstances. Down the passage a cell door opened and Anderson came staggering out, gaunt, hollow-eyed and bearded.

'Gaston!' he exclaimed hoarsely.

'Yes, it's me, Anderson. I've done irreparable damage, and this is a slight effort to atone for it. That damnable vibrator has jammed — is running perpetually on its own power. It hasn't a water generator, or else it would have stopped long ago. For God's sake, stop it!'

Anderson clutched the ex-servant's shoulder. 'But even if I stop it now, the atomic disruption will go on!'

Gaston nodded weakly. 'True. But when the last atom of dust has exploded, there will be no more disruptions if that instrument is shut off. Dust will gather again and settle, and the world of men will return. Go on, Anderson, do it — save the world of the future at least. I'm — done!' And with the words Gaston collapsed to the floor.

'You're not leaving here; we must have proof of your sanity first,' snapped the supervisor.

'Proof be damned!' Anderson snarled, swinging round on him. 'I'll give you a proof such as no man has ever had before. Come with me — give me this one chance. Bring straitjackets, guns, re-volvers — anything else you like, and if you're not satisfied when I've finished, you can lock me up for life. Now come on.'

And not ten minutes later a powerful car swept out of the asylum drive toward the abode of the late Professor Renhard — the man who had stopped the dust.

★   ★   ★

'The blackness has ceased!' Sam Brown exclaimed suddenly, pointing upward. 'We win, my friends! We win! See — the blue is spreading very slowly — already the dust is spreading outward — giving us back our blue sky — our world of men!'

In silence the others looked upward, all unaware that at that identical moment in London Dr. Anderson had stopped the outflow of power from the vibrator. Instantly Sam's counteracter was able to exert to its full effect.

'Yes — we win!' Sam said again, in a voice of triumph.

And those were the last words he ever uttered.

For, quite abruptly, as the blueness, began to spread, it seemed as though the pink screen suddenly warped and bent downward. There came a blinding blue flash from the instruments and a terrific explosion that tore up the ground for a mile in every direction. Men, apparatus, planes, instruments — all vanished in fragments — but the blue sky still spread, bringing back normalcy to a tortured world.

For with all his careful calculations, with all the careful checking of his figures, Sam Brown had forgotten one thing. The hurling forth of the negative power to stop the explosion of atoms would entail a recoil effect thousands of times greater than that of firing a shell from a big gun. Hence the recoil had compressed itself into the useless confines of the instruments, and blown them — and the men — to fragments.

2

Rim of Eternity

'Nothing really exists,' declared Professor Engleman, with due academic profundity. 'That, of course, may sound preposterous, but it is nevertheless a fact and I am sure that the members of this erudite gathering know exactly what I mean.'

Yes, everybody knew what he meant, but it was becoming increasingly difficult to concentrate. For one thing, the great lecture hall where Engleman was holding forth was intolerably stuffy; for another there were all the attractions of a warm summer evening beckoning outside. Not far from the lecture hall lay the Great Park, in the grounds of which the hall itself stood. Through the open windows floated the sound of children's laughter, the clack of cricket balls, even the distant sonorous strains of an open-air brass band.

Professor Engleman had been asked to

demonstrate to members of the scientific profession his latest discoveries concerning the electron. This suited Engleman — who never knew what the weather was like anyway — down to the ground. But it made it tough going for his hearers who were compelled to be present.

'Nothing really exists because everything is based on the electron, and the electron itself is only a probability,' Engleman continued, without resorting to his notes. 'No scientist can say positively, even today, that an electron exists as a unit of electricity: he can only *infer* that it does because all mathematical laws point to its presence. But we cannot *see* it, my friends! The very action of even trying to do so, in bringing light-waves upon it to discover it, is enough to deflect it out of sight. Hence, I say, all existence — which of necessity is based on electrons — is nothing more than a probability. As such it is a completely unstable state . . .'

'Hear, hear,' murmured an elder savant dutifully, and peered through sleepy eyes at the little, sixty-year old doyen of electronics who was responsible for this boring recital of known facts.

'To prove my point — and, I hope, usher in a new theory concerning electronics — I have here a machine . . . ' Engleman indicated it standing on a massive table to one side of the rostrum. The apparatus looked like a glorified telephone switchboard with two tubes on the summit.

'With it,' Engleman continued, 'it is possible to set up a disturbing electrical field which will so displace the electrons of matter as to cause their atomic constitution to form entirely new patterns. My equations tell me that, as a result of this, certain species of matter can cease to exist altogether, whilst others can assume new shapes. How far the influence of this disturber-field reaches I do not know. My study of it shows it seems to have no limit but spreads out in an ever-widening circle. Possibly, even, it may reach to the limits of the Universe and then start to contract inwards again. One thing *is* certain: the outward speed of the field is many times greater than that of light . . . '

A certain sense of uneasiness crept over the members. It was just possible that the old boy in his enthusiasm might dissipate the entire hall and its living inhabitants. His genius was such that the possibility of his having invented a failure was unthinkable. Then his next words brought relief.

'Fortunately, the control of the disturber-field is absolute. I can automatically set it to operate at ten feet or ten miles as the mood dictates. I have therefore set it tonight for a distance of exactly seven and a half miles — which, I am assured on the high authority of the Borough Surveyor, is the exact distance from this hall to St. Michael's statue.'

There was a murmur of assent. St. Michael's statue stood in a great, deserted space on the edge of London. It had been erected by some obscure religious denomination as a silent exhortation to infidels to heed more closely the Voice of Reason.

'I propose,' Engleman proceeded, 'to see what happens to that statue when the disturber-field reaches it. I have only to press the switch on this machine and the job is done. We can then set off and see for ourselves what has happened to St. Michael.'

To this the reaction was unanimously in favour since it meant a jaunt through the summer evening and an exodus of the stifling lecture hall.

'I hope,' Engelman murmured, studying his apparatus, 'that all is well with this equipment. I was compelled to entrust it to the tender mercies of the carriers in order to get it here, it being too large to fit into my private car. Mmm, yes, all seems to be in order.'

He peered short-sightedly at the dials and controls, and saw nothing wrong. Not that there was — at least not visibly. There were, however, certain differences in the internal workings, brought about entirely by the ruthless manhandling of the carriers who had dumped the equipment with complete lack of regard for its extreme sensitivity.

'All I have to do,' Engleman said, 'is press this button here, which immediately starts the emanation of the disturber-wave.'

In the centre of Great Park an old man of eighty-seven sat studying a pocket Bible. In spite of his age he was fairly well preserved. His back was still upright: he held the Book in hands that did not tremble. Seated as he was on the rustic seat built round the bole of a giant cedar tree, the mid-evening sunlight casting a halo through his silver hair, there was something immensely venerable about him. He seemed apart from everything, lost in his assiduous study of the Scriptures.

The gambolling children nearby took no notice of him, but once or twice a young woman, perhaps twenty-two, sprawled alone on the grass, cast a sly glance in his direction. She was pretty, shapely, and appeared to have everything a girl of her age should have. It was not possible for her to go round with a label proclaiming she had only three months to live because of the inexorable inroads of galloping consumption.

Whilst she cast covert glances at the old man, seeing in him something saintly, something perhaps which could drag her from the death sentence passed upon her, she too was also under observation, though she was not aware of it.

A few yards away from her a young man was sprawled against a tree, a wisp of grass between his teeth. He was good looking, but hard about the mouth and grim around the eyes. Back of his mind was the contemplation of murder — this very night. He meant to snuff out a young woman who had completely misled him as to her intentions. Once that was done . . . well, here was another young woman, alone, extremely pretty. Pity she coughed so much, but probably a few throat pastilles could cure that.

'Not bad,' Martin Senior muttered to himself lazily. 'Not bad at all. Give it a bit longer and then accidentally fall over her feet as you leave. Corny introduction but better than nothing!'

He knew exactly in his own mind what he intended doing. But, even as Professor Engleman was at that very moment pointing out, nobody can be sure of anything, because nothing really exists. There is only the probability that a thing exists . . .

And, divided by only a scant fifty yards from these three characters and the laughing, then squabbling, children, there lay the tennis courts. The evening was too hot for anybody but enthusiasts, and into this class fell Jerry Maxbury and Edna Drew. They had been slogging at one another for over an hour, and from the look on the girl's face she did not at all like the battering she was getting.

'All very well for you!' she shouted indignantly, as she lost game, set and match and threw down her racquet savagely. 'You've got legs a mile long and a reach like a giraffe! How am I supposed to stand up to that?'

'You're not supposed to,' Jerry grinned, vaulting the net and hurrying to her side. 'Somebody's got to win, Ed, and it may as well be me!'

'Beast!' Edna looked at him under her eyes, her lips pouting. She was a dark girl of average looks, usually marred by an expression of sullen resignation. Jerry, on the other hand, was a Nordic blond, the kind a teenager might swoon for — only

Jerry was not interested in teenagers: only in Edna.

'You don't have to take it so hard,' he complained, tying his sweater about his neck and then retrieving her racquet for her. 'That's the trouble with us, Ed: we never seem to agree, and yet we somehow stick together. Maybe we're getting all our quarrels over before we get married.'

'If we ever do!' Edna retorted and strode away angrily in the direction of the Tennis Club pavilion. Jerry sighed as he watched her go, but the slim lines of her figure in the sleeveless tennis frock drew him after her. Nearby the Park clock struck nine-fifteen.

He caught up with her at the pavilion counter. In here was the 'honour counter' whereby drinks, sweets and confectionery could be obtained, the payment to be placed in a special box. Whether the idea worked or not was nobody's concern: on the whole the club membership was straightforward enough.

'Now, look — ' Jerry began, and then he could not say any, more because the thing happened.

He and Edna were suddenly flat on their backs, their brains and senses stunned by an inconceivable impact. They were transiently dead and yet in full possession of their faculties. They just lay, fixedly watching a blinding whirl of lights outside the pavilion windows. There was a monstrous sucking noise like an elephant going down in a bog. This terminated in a violent explosion that made the pavilion windows rattle — then all was quiet again.

Jerry stirred slowly, gradually struggled to his feet. With a dazed look in his eyes he lifted Edna beside him. Fright had completely destroyed her earlier anger.

'What — what was it, do you suppose?' Her dark eyes were racing with questions.

'Hanged if I know. Earthquake or something. Or maybe the much vaunted X-bomb has dropped at last.'

He went to the pavilion's open doorway and gazed outside; then he nearly fainted from shock. Simultaneously he felt Edna's convulsive grip on his arm.

'Lord!' she gasped. 'Oh, Lord!'

For some reason the Great Park had

entirely vanished! Instead the pavilion seemed to be perched on some kind of desert island, only instead of there being ocean beyond the very near horizon there were stars! Stars set in a sky of violent blue. Wherever Jerry and Edna looked there were the stars. Right behind the pavilion itself there was a sheer drop into — infinity itself! Stars were behind, above, below!

'We're dead — or dreaming!' Jerry whispered at last.

'But not alone, thank heaven. Look — there are others!'

Jerry saw them now. Not far away were two big trees, looking ridiculously lonely and adding to the 'desert island' effect. Under one of them sat an old man with silver hair; under the other was a young man, now rising to his feet and looking about him. In the middle distance a pretty young woman lay sprawled on the grass, one hand holding down the hem of her skirt as a brief hot wind gushed past and was gone.

'Hey!' Jerry yelled. 'Hey, you folks! What happened?'

The young man began to advance, hesitated, and instead turned to help the girl to her feet. Then they both moved to the old man as he struggled up from the rustic bench around the cedar tree. After a moment all three came slowly forward, the younger ones held back in their urgency by the old man's slow progress.

It struck Jerry as he watched them that everything was brightly lighted. The sun, of course. The sun? He glanced upwards again at the multitude of stars and realized the oddity of the situation. There was a sun up there, certainly, only it had a blueish instead of amber light. Also it was at the zenith, whereas it had been evening before this — whatever it was — had happened.

'What happened?' It was Edna's urgent voice as the 'outside' trio came up the pavilion steps. 'We didn't see. We were in here.'

'I just don't know what did happen,' Martin Senior answered. 'I was just lying there, thinking of this and that — then everything seemed to abruptly fly apart and snap together again, quick as a flash.

Then I found myself looking at stars.'

'Same as me:' the consumptive girl said, her gray eyes wide in amazement. 'Where's the Park? The kids who were playing? In fact where is anything?'

''And in the twinkling of an eye all shall be changed',' the old man murmured, shaking his white head slowly. 'Y'know, I never thought I'd live to see that really happen. And if you don't mind I'll sit down. My legs aren't what they used to be.'

'Sure,' Jerry agreed promptly, settling him on the pavilion steps. 'Make yourself comfortable, sir, whilst we work out what's happened.'

The old man glanced up with tired amusement in his blue eyes. 'You think you can? The optimism of youth!'

'Well, there has to be an explanation, of course.' Jerry reflected for a moment. 'Now, let me see — '

'We're on some kind of asteroid, I think,' Martin Senior interrupted. 'Or, more precisely, a segment of Earth has broken away from the parent body, and we happened to be on it. Where we are now, God knows.'

'God always knows,' the old man said, musing. 'And a grand mess we'd all be in if He didn't.'

'I find that sort of remark both irrelevant and unhelpful,' Edna snapped. 'This is a desperately serious situation. We're utterly marooned, and we don't know where!'

'Take it easy,' Jerry growled. 'Things are tough enough without you blowing your top!'

'Then suggest something!' Edna spread her slim bare arms and glared.

Silence. The men looked at one another and the two young women exchanged glances. Finally Jerry cleared his throat.

'Your idea of a segment of Earth flying away and taking us with it is too Arabian Nightish,' he declared, looking frankly at Martin Senior. 'I'm not a scientist, but I do know it could not happen. We're breathing air for one thing, and in a case like that we wouldn't be. The air would be sucked like — like skin from a banana.'

'It wouldn't be if the change were *instantaneous*, involving no momentum.

Just a switch from place to place.'

'Eh?' Jerry stared blankly. 'But that couldn't happen!'

'Fact remains, it did.' Martin Senior looked at the starry sky. 'Notice something? None of those stars form constellations that make sense. And also that sun isn't ours at all. It's bluer, younger, and hotter. We're in a totally unknown area of space!'

'Perhaps,' the consumptive girl ventured, 'the rest of the world is here just the same only we can't see it for some reason?'

Martin Senior shook his head. 'That is belied by the slight gravity we now have. You must have noticed it — I feel feather light, and so must the rest of you.'

At which Jerry gathered himself together and then jumped. He seemed to travel right to the edge of the near horizon before he landed.

'You're right!' he yelled back.

'Come back!' Edna screamed hysterically. 'You'll fall off into — that emptiness there!'

Jerry came back in prodigious leaps. 'No chance of it, Ed, any more than you could fall off the Earth itself.'

Edna looked out into the starry silences, a desperately bewildered young woman. The same frightened, lonely look was in the eyes of the consumptive girl, too. The two younger men were trying to look self-assured but the mystification in their eyes could not be hidden. Only the old man seemed undisturbed, sitting as calmly as a weather-beaten old fisherman watching a sunset.

'This,' he said, brooding, 'gives us the chance to look at ourselves, to decide how much we really count in the scheme of things. It's a wonderful opportunity!'

Edna hugged her elbows and shivered. 'Then it's an opportunity in which I'm not interested. Look, do you others find it cold? Wish to heaven my coat was here. I left it on the chair beside the tennis court.'

Nobody said anything. The tennis court! It might be millions of light centuries away. Might even be in another space altogether. Here there was nothing but infinity, the violent sky, the silly gravitation, and a sun that had no right to be there.

'Come to think of it,' Martin Senior said presently, 'it is getting cold, or else we got steamed up with fright and are now cooling off. Let's get into the pavilion and try and knock some sense into things.'

His hard, matter-of-fact logic was just what was wanted at that moment. Edna and the consumptive girl followed him into the pavilion and seated themselves. Jerry stayed long enough to give the old man a hand; then with the doors closed they settled and considered one another.

'First things first,' Martin Senior said, his law very square and determined. 'I'm Martin Senior, engineer's draughtsman.'

'Lucille Grant,' the consumptive girl said, and looked anxiously about her.

Each in turn Jerry and Edna introduced themselves and then the old man smiled and sighed.

'What's in a name anyhow?' he shrugged. 'My name's Jonathan Stone, and I'm a retired publisher. I've reached the age when I've about done everything there is to do. Where I end my life doesn't signify, be it in this incredible place or in bed at home. I'm prepared to let the good Lord make the arrangements.'

'At your age you can't see it as we see it,' Edna insisted.

'Speak for yourself,' Lucille put in. 'I can see things exactly the same way as Mr. Stone. What does it matter anyway?'

Jonathan Stone looked at her fixedly. 'Strange words from a girl your age. What are you? Twenty-five maybe?'

'Twenty-two, but I'll never be twenty-three. The doctors have told me that.'

'Come to think of it,' Martin Senior said dryly, 'we'll none of us live for long if we don't find the way home — and I don't think we've the remotest chance of doing that.'

'Talk, talk, talk!' Edna beat her fists fiercely on her knees. 'I always thought men came up with something brilliant in a crisis — and you spend your time talking rubbish! What do we *do*?'

'We've nothing to go on,' Jerry protested. 'And stop being so difficult, Ed. Things are bad enough . . . '

'We can only assume certain facts,' Martin Senior said, his tone coldly calculating. 'Some scientific process, or else natural forces, has hurled us on a fragment of Earth into unknown space. The transition was instantaneous for two reasons. We were aware of it and didn't lose consciousness, and our air came with us. Further, it was smooth and untroubled because the pavilion and the two trees remain firm. They were not uprooted and flung into chaos. We heard a violent explosion after a sucking noise. That could have been our air racing outwards and the gap closing behind. We know also we have travelled an incomprehensible distance because our own sun had disappeared, and we have a different one. Right so far?'

Heads nodded silently — all except Jonathan Stone's. He was not even listening. Instead he was pondering his small pocket Bible.

'And the time now is . . . ' Martin Senior considered his watch. 'Er — nine-thirty. Fifteen minutes ago we were in the Great Park on Earth and everything was perfect. No amount of reasoning or logic or anything else can explain a vast trip through infinity in the space of what must have been seconds. We just don't know what has happened.'

'Could it reverse itself and take us back?' Jerry asked, pondering.

'No idea. You're as wise as I am. It would take an Einstein to work this one out.'

'Can an ex-high school girl say something?' Edna enquired. 'I once learned the fact that you cannot take anything away from the Universe's structure without putting something in its place. Therefore — '

'Matter into energy; energy into matter,' Martin Senior confirmed calmly. 'So?'

'Just this. We must have left something behind when we departed. I mean, a great chunk of Earth couldn't vanish abruptly without something taking its place.'

'Possibly the interchange was absolute,' Martin Senior mused. 'By that I mean that we abruptly changed places with another part of the universe; therefore whatever was here is now where we were. Maybe it was empty space, maybe a star, maybe anything. If a star, then Earth by now will be a cinder.'

Silence. Jerry turned and looked at the

'honour counter' with the banked-up shelves behind it. He gave a sigh.

'Well, there's a certain amount of food and drink here which will keep us going for awhile. When it runs out that's the finish.'

'To my mind . . . ' Martin Senior got to his feet. 'To my mind I think we should explore this desert island segment of ours more thoroughly.'

'Okay,' Jerry nodded. 'I'll come with you — '

'No you won't!' Edna interrupted. 'You're staying right by me, Jerry! I'm scared! Mr. Stone's too old to be of any help if anything happens and — '

'I'll go,' Lucille said, with a touch of contempt, getting to her feet. 'That is if you think a woman is capable of revealing any commonsense, Mr. Senior?'

Martin Senior only smiled sardonically and then opened the pavilion door, following Lucille out into the blaze of the alien sun. They descended the steps with queer, bouncing movements and then began to cross the grass together.

'I could laugh,' Martin Senior exclaimed,

after a moment. 'I really could!'

'So could I, for another reason.' Lucille gave him a quick look. 'I've about three months to live and find myself here! I never thought I'd watch others die around me at the same time.'

'You seem mighty sure that you're going to push up the daisies!'

'That's rather a fatuous remark here, isn't it? And of course I'm sure. No reason why the medics should lie to me.'

'Not necessarily lie, but they're not infallible. Believe only in yourself and nobody else. That's my motto.'

'I wish I could, but I'm not made that way.' Lucille looked about her towards the very near horizon. Then: 'And what was it was going to make you laugh?'

'Just the fact that I'd planned to murder a girl tonight! Now she's light centuries away and perfectly safe. A classic example of 'Man proposes . . . ' I suppose.'

'You? Commit a murder? I don't believe it!'

'Thanks for the compliment. And, Miss Grant, unless I am permitted to call you

Lucille, we are now leaving the pavilion right behind us.'

Lucille stopped and glanced rearward. Then she gave a start. The top of the pavilion roof was visible, but that was all. The rest of it was below the horizon.

'This is preposterous!' she exclaimed, startled.

'Not a bit. We just happen to have walked beyond the horizon point — as seen from the pavilion, that is. Notice the ground? The grass has finished and instead we we have this stuff! Soil, but flat as though a roller had been over it.'

'So it is!' Lucille looked at it intently. 'Looks as if a giant knife had cut it off.'

They began moving again, and behind them the pavilion slowly vanished from view. They were now traversing a twilit plain of perfectly smooth soil on which no living thing grew. Overhead were the stars, but no sun.

'This segment we're on is only quite small,' Martin Senior said presently. 'At the moment we're on its underside, which is why the sun's gone.'

'Which means we're upside down

compared to our position in the pavilion?'

'Of course, but we're not aware of it because gravity keeps us apparently upright. No doubt of one thing, this clean-cut segment points to colossal elemental forces. This piece of Earth wasn't just ripped out: it was sheared off!'

'Couldn't be!'

'It could, though I'm not scientist enough to imagine how. Did you ever see anything so absolutely flat?'

They gazed over the expanse to the near horizon. Not a hillock, not an undulation, anywhere. Overhead the strange, unknown stars and the everlasting black of space itself. Somewhere, faded as a forgotten memory, was the world from which they had come.

'We can assess this by degrees,' Martin Senior said, thinking. 'We're on a chunk of Earth approximately three miles long by — say, two wide. It makes no pretence of being circular: it's plainly and simply a chunk. The upper part is normal with grass, trees, the pavilion, and so on: the under part is sheared off where the mysterious forces went to work. Air we still have — but it can't last.'

'Why not?' Lucille asked, that depthless wonder still in her eyes.

'For one thing the gravity is so weak it won't hold the air for long; for another space will suck it out gradually. Also, the best of the sun will do its share to dissipating it. How long we have I don't know.' Martin Senior surveyed the stars. 'They're very bright. Our atmosphere here is desperately thin — or maybe you'd noticed? That tightness about the chest?'

'My chest's always tight anyway so I wouldn't know — ' Lucille broke off in a fit of coughing. When at last it had subsided she was surprised to find Martin Senior's arm about her shoulders.

'Better?' he asked, with a kind of rough kindness.

'Uh-uh: it comes in spasms. We'd better be getting back and tell the others, hadn't we?'

Martin Senior nodded, and they retraced their way. They found the others still in the pavilion, Edna being in the midst of rationing what food there was.

She glanced up at the two entered.

'Well?'

Martin Senior shrugged. 'Nothing very exciting — except proof of the fact that our island home was pitched here by scientific forces . . . ' and he briefly added the details.

'Very helpful,' Edna commented sourly, slapping down a spot of shrimp paste. 'At least you both managed to cultivate a good sunburn, anyhow!'

'Edna, for heaven's sake!' Jerry gave her an entreating look.

'For heaven's sake what? I can speak my mind, can't I?'

'I have the feeling,' Jonathan Stone remarked, his spare form reclining in the wicker chair by the sunlit window, 'that Miss Drew is not at all happy in her present surroundings!'

'Are you?' Edna demanded.

'Quite — but then I have reached the age where I can be philosophical. Out here we're somehow right on the rim of Eternity, and I have the hope that before I die I might even look upon the face of my Creator.'

Because of his age, Jonathan Stone's statement did not sound at all blasphemous: indeed, the serene expression on his rugged old face made it appear that he really believed his wish would be granted.

'To get to more practical things,' Martin Senior said bluntly, 'we've fallen into an orbit. I've been watching the stars, and they're changing position very slightly where as the sun doesn't move in the least. That suggests that we're flying round this sun and keeping one face to it. Fortunate it happens to be this one or we'd be completely in the dark.'

'We are — utterly!' Edna Drew's mouth was drooping peevishly. 'It's cold, frightening, and desolate. If there were not you others here I'd go mad!'

'Put my sweater on . . . ' Jerry handed it across.

'No thanks. I can look after myself. Serves me right for putting on this fool tennis frock without sleeves in it. But how was I to know this would happen?'

'We none of us knew,' Jonathan Stone said. ''In the twinkling of an eye — '!'

'So you said before,' Edna interrupted

rudely. 'Surely, Mr. Stone, at your age, you can contribute something more useful to our dilemma than mere Scriptures?'

'I am afraid not, Miss Drew. I am too old physically to do anything, and mentally I am more preoccupied with the Hereafter than the present.'

'As to the coldness . . . ' Martin Senior reached down a packet of cigarettes from the shelf. 'That's caused by the air here being unpleasantly thin. It causes rapid radiation of bodily warmth and causes the surface skin to chill quickly. You won't catch cold, though, because that takes germs — and I doubt if they're very prevalent on this remote chunk of Earth; or even if they are the thin air won't encourage them.'

Edna threw herself onto one of the counter stools and looked moodily in front of her. She ignored the cigarette packet Martin Senior held towards her: Lucille also declined as another violent attack of coughing brought her to the point of exhaustion.

'I think,' Edna said curtly, when the

spasm had finished, 'that it might be healthier outside. Come on, Jerry!'

'Why?' He was squatting comfortably on the floor, smoking one of the cigarettes Martin Senior had offered him.

'Because I refuse to venture out alone.'

Jerry sighed and scrambled to his feet. He paused as he went past Lucille. She was still gasping for breath and the paroxysms had brought tears to her wide gray eyes.

'Sorry, Lucille, for what Edna said,' he murmured. 'I don't think she meant it. Sort of prides herself on being outspoken.'

'Of course,' Lucille smiled. 'If I could help myself coughing I would.'

'For heaven's sake come on and stop muttering!' Edna complained — so Jerry hurried quickly to her side and then followed her to the open. The three left behind gazed after them.

'Not ideally suited, are they?' Martin Senior asked cynically.

'Few people are,' Jonathan Stone sighed. 'I think they'd get along all right if they could compose the antagonisms in their natures. Each has something the other cannot assimilate, and until they find out what it is they'll always be at loggerheads.'

'About the sunburn we've got — ' Lucille seemed to have been thinking, and she was now inspecting the undoubted chocolate brown on the backs of her normally pale hands. 'Isn't that caused by ultra-violet radiation?'

'Normally, yes,' Martin Senior confirmed. 'This new sun we've got probably radiates ultra-violet the same as our own does, but here we get the dose extra strong because of the thin air. On the other hand, it may not be ultra violet at all.'

'It must be to produce sunburn!' Lucille insisted.

'Not necessarily. Cosmic rays could produce the same effect, and much more rapidly. Indeed, considering the speed at which we have got bronzed I'm inclined to think cosmic rays are at the back of it.'

'But they're dangerous!' Lucille exclaimed. 'I've read about them! They burn flesh and blood and go right through everything except lead.'

'True enough — in the naked state. We have some atmosphere to shield us — ' Martin Senior broke off and then nodded towards the almost sleeping Jonathan Stone. 'There's our proof! Mr. Stone is becoming sunburned, too, and he hasn't been outside the pavilion yet — except at the very start. That shows the cosmic radiations are passing through this pavilion, something which ultra-violet cannot do. Come to think of it, Jerry and Edna looked remarkably healthy, but I put it down to their having been playing tennis in the sun.'

'That sounds an awful long way off now,' Lucille whispered.

After a while Jerry and Edna returned. They were still looking at odds with each other — and the increase in their 'sunburn' was most marked. Moodily they came into the pavilion and then closed the door.

'According to my watch it's half-past twelve,' Jerry said. 'Back home that would be long past bedtime and by all the rules I ought to feel sleepy. But I don't — and neither does Edna.'

Martin Senior looked vaguely surprised. 'Come to think of it, I don't either. How about you, Lucille?'

'A bit — but not as much as usual.'

'The only one who seems to be running to schedule is Mr. Stone,' Jerry commented, glancing at him. 'Fast asleep!'

'Don't you believe it, boy!' The old man stirred and looked at him. 'Because I have my eyes closed doesn't say I'm asleep. Matter of fact I don't feel tired. In fact quite the contrary. Surprising thing, but since we landed here I've felt immeasurably younger.'

'The air perhaps,' Edna said, but she did not sound too certain of herself. 'It's a bit thin, but immensely exhilarating. I don't feel cold any more either.'

There was silence for a moment. Though as yet none was prepared to admit it — except perhaps for Jonathan Stone — they were all conscious of alerted senses, of the slow dissolution of that stagnation of the mind that more or less pervades every human being through the action of impurities in blood. Thinking seemed no longer a conscious effort: the concentration flew from one topic to another with astonishing facility.

'Sunburn and sharpened wits, eh?' Martin Senior asked at length. 'Only one answer to that — the inflow of cosmic radiation affecting us all.'

Jonathan Stone chuckled half to himself. 'Good for you, son! You have your answer — and I have mine.'

'You mean you have a different solution?'

'I wouldn't say it's a solution, but at any rate it's a suggestion. Just here, in this unknown region of space, we may be much closer to the Ultimate than we were on Earth. And by the Ultimate I mean the Artisan of the Universe, the Creator of all that is — '

'He's off again,' Edna sighed, sitting down. 'Just as I thought we were going to pin something down.'

The old man looked at her reprovingly. 'Trouble with you youngsters is you don't pay half enough attention to spiritual values — '

'For myself,' Martin Senior interrupted, with an immense calm, 'I'm an incisive, calculating man with no interest in spiritual values. You could call me an atheist even, and be quite correct. Therefore I say that the presence of cosmic rays, which are everywhere in the Universe, is the main cause of the slow change which is coming upon us. It is not, I contend, because we are nearer to some hypothetical Creator.'

'You have your view, and I have mine,' Stone smiled. 'The Bible tells us that the power of the Creator is everywhere — everywhere! So are cosmic radiations. Is it impossible to draw a connection between the two? No scientist will positively tell you whence cosmic rays emanate because he doesn't know the answer. That they are caused by the breakdown or build-up of energy in remote parts of space doesn't settle the issue. They have always been there: they always will be there — steady, unvarying, ubiquitous. They are material — '

'Therefore not spiritual,' Martin Senior snapped.

'Not necessarily. We are mortal beings accustomed to interpret everything from its material basis. The power of a Creator might, to us, appear as cosmic radiation — destructive, deadly. To one with clearer vision they could represent the beneficent outflow of a Creator, and here at this remote point of space we may be nearer to that source of all-intellect, all-power, than ever before. Also, being segregated from our own kind with the disturbance of their myriads of conflicting thoughts, we are able to think and apprehend clearly for the first time in our lives. At least I am.'

Silence. Lucille stared blankly, too astonished to make any comment. Edna was smiling cynically yet with a half doubt in her eyes. Martin Senior lighted a cigarette and sucked in a mouthful of fumes. Jerry looked about him and then rubbed the back of his neck.

'Frankly, I don't get it,' he confessed.

The old man opened his pocket Bible and considered it. 'You would, son, if you'd studied this a bit more often. No, no, I'm not censuring you. At your age I was just as carefree. You still have time to catch up.'

Edna got to her feet with the decisiveness of disgust. She gave Jerry a glance.

'About time we had something to eat, isn't it?'

Jerry hesitated. 'I suppose so, but somehow I — I don't want it. I'm not hungry. That isn't the aftermath of shock either: it's just that I never felt less inclined for food in all my life.'

Edna looked at the others. 'What about you folks?'

Each one shook their heads, at which she moved to the nearby piled-up rations and began to make selections. Then after a while she paused and slowly shook her head. She turned, a puzzled light in her dark eyes.

'Whatever it is it's got me too. I've no appetite — nor am I thirsty either.'

'Now you know how the Ancients managed to fast for weeks on end without harm,' Jonathan Stone commented. 'They had the trick of utilizing spiritual power for their sustenance — an art submerged with the materialistic centuries which followed.'

'Which, interpreted, means that the cosmic rays are feeding us?' Martin Senior asked bluntly. 'Just as they fed the Ancients?'

'Your interpretation is correct, Mr. Senior.'

'It's crazy! Idiotic!' Martin Senior spat out his cigarette and then stamped on it. 'Cosmic rays destroy: they don't feed!'

'None of us is destroyed, though,' Lucille pointed out gently. 'In fact we all look a good deal better than when we arrived here. How do you account for that?'

'They just can't be cosmic rays, that's all. Something else.'

'You don't believe that,' Jerry said deliberately. 'Out here in these wastes nothing else but cosmic rays could affect us. We wouldn't be as affected as we are by ultra-violet, seventh-octave radiations, or any of those.'

Edna came forward in surprise. 'How in the world do you know all that? I never heard you make a scientific statement in your life before.'

'I — I don't quite know. It sort of came to me.'

'The whole thing is perfectly simple to analyze . . . ' Jonathan Stone rose from the wicker chair — not awkwardly under the cramp of age, but with the litheness of a young man. 'Cosmic radiation and Creative power are one and the same thing: that is my contention. Scientists aver that cosmic radiation, in the Beginning, acted as a catalyst on certain chemical substances, and so life began. Very well: they're entitled to their material conception of life's beginning. We are also told that the Creator brought life into being by His emanations and beneficence. The two things — cosmic rays material, and emanations spiritual — could be one and the same. Science proves cosmic rays to be destructive to life. But suppose everybody had been educated through the centuries to believe that they are beneficial to life? What then?'

'They would be,' Lucille said quickly, her eyes bright. 'Every single one of us believes a thing because we are compelled to from the cradle. Believe otherwise and — '

'You'd get whatever you believe,' Stone assented, smiling at her. 'The old quotation — 'There is nothing either good or bad but thinking makes it so' is a profound truth. Now, to get to our point. Here there are only five of us, utterly removed from the mass opinions of multimillions of our fellow human beings. Their thoughts no longer cloud our minds: we are so far away from them we are unaffected by them. So we receive cosmic rays — or spiritual radiations — or whatever you like to call them, as they really are. We have no preconceived opinions about them: there are no educational beliefs to be overcome. We accept them and they are beneficent.'

Martin Senior smiled oddly. 'We talk indeed from the heights of Olympus, Mr. Stone — yet withal I can detect the logic of your argument. I am one who relies on proof, and in this case the proof is that we are not hurt in any way by this all-inclusive radiation that is pouring down on us with every second. That is enough for me. There remains the problem of what happens next. To have

105

perhaps solved the conditions existing here does not by any means tell us how we get home.'

'Do we want to?' Jonathan Stone turned and looked through the pavilion window, the eternal sunlight again casting a halo around his white hair. 'Don't you feel, here on this outermost rim of the Universe, that we are nearer our chosen destiny than we ever could be back on Earth? The freedom of thought, the well-being of the body: those attributes I would never trade for the old life back on Earth.'

'Well-being of the body,' Lucille repeated slowly, and then smiled wryly. 'From where I'm sitting, Mr. Stone, that has a decid-edly ironic ring. I'm a doomed woman — or didn't I mention it?'

'Because of incurable illness?' Stone turned to look at hers 'That was back on Earth, child. Are you sure your viewpoint is still correct, or have cosmic rays destroyed the trouble which was undermining you?'

Lucille hesitated and then looked down at herself, clearly uncertain. Martin Senior looked at her also, an odd expression in his sharp eyes.

'It's a long time since you coughed,' he said.

'That's nothing. Sometimes I go for days on end without any trouble. Just the same . . . ' Lucille hesitated, distance in her eyes. 'Just the same, I do feel different somehow.'

Edna moved restlessly. 'Conversations always bore me,' she confessed. 'And since sleep and food both seem written off I think I'll go for another walk. I'm even inclined to believe that there may be something in what you say, Mr. Stone. I'd like to think it out.'

'By all means.'

Edna turned pensively towards the door, then Jerry's voice gave her pause.

'Just a moment, Ed! I thought you were afraid to go out alone?'

'I was. Somehow I'm not any more. Still, if you want to come with me by all means do so!'

Jerry did not hesitate. For the second time since they had so mysteriously arrived in this alien region the two who could not understand each other — and yet felt impelled towards each other — wandered, out under the brittle stars.

★   ★   ★

Jonathan Stone had hit the nail on the head — and not entirely by accident either. His great age, his years of study of the profundities of life and mind, had in some subtle way groomed him for this moment, wherein he was positioned as a kind of revelator. He knew, with everything that was in him, that his theory of the dual nature of cosmic rays was right. It must be right for cosmic rays are everywhere. There is no place where they are not. Of the power of a Creator the same thing can be stated. Such a parallel could not possibly be coincidence.

And with every moment, every second, these invisible radiations were beating down from their unknown source, bereft of their deadly qualities because there were no influencing minds present to produce a material effect contrary to the normal one. So five people lost in the Universe, through the unintentional meddling of an aged

108

University professor, were swiftly changing — following the course normal to the absorption of cosmic rays, and were evolving. Swiftly! Incredibly!

Not only those in the pavilion were aware of it, but Edna and Jerry also. Indeed, for them, the effect was if anything much swifter because there was no slight deflection of radiations from the pavilion roof.

'I have often wondered,' Jerry said seriously, when he and Edna had come to the last grass knoll separating them from the 'soil plain' on the fragment's other side, 'what it must feel like to have godlike power. Now I know.'

Edna had no bitter response to make this time. She accepted his words as absolute fact because she felt exactly as he did. In silence they both stood on the slight rise of grassy ground looking upwards towards the stars.

'Whatever it is that is the source of cosmic rays, be it material or spiritual, it's definitely up there — or out there,' Jerry said slowly. 'Can't you feel that? Far more so than the last time we came out here?'

Edna was silent for a moment, erect, her head thrown back as she stared aloft.

'I more than feel it, Jerry, I see it. Something — out there — incredibly bright and yet so infinitely gentle — '

Jerry did not answer. He could not sense exactly what Edna meant. Manlike, he could not even hope to realize that at that moment Edna was undergoing a complete transformation. As a woman, hard-surfaced though she had been, she had the innate qualities of conception, which Jerry could never possess. Yet even he glimpsed something for a moment. It seemed like a shaft of pearly radiance, evanescent, unthinkably lovely, projected straight out of the void down towards this hurtling, forgotten little fragment of Earth. For a moment even it looked as though both he and Edna were washed in cold fire . . . Then it was gone, but it had left behind the breath of genius.

'Somehow — somehow, Ed — ' Jerry stumbled over his words. 'Somehow I know now why we've never agreed. Our physical make-ups have been opposed. We've had mathematical strains in each of us that have cancelled each other out, making absolute unison impossible.'

'Yes,' Edna assented simply. 'That's the answer. But now it doesn't exist because in that moment the mathematical strains straightened. The complexities which separated us, and yet attracted, have been resolved.'

They looked at each other, god and goddess without realizing it. Mentally they had grown to immeasurable stature, had almost reached the stage of absolute evolution as far as their minds were concerned. Their bodies had responded in that they were young, lithe, bronzed, of superlative physique.

'It has been worth coming here if only to resolve those differences,' Jerry smiled. 'We'll never misunderstand one another again. Suppose we get back and tell the others?'

Before long they had returned to the pavilion, to discover about Stone, Martin Senior, and Lucille a certain radiant assurance that spoke for itself.

'We felt we should tell you what happened to us out there!' Jerry exclaimed eagerly. 'We saw something, and somehow felt it too — then afterwards our misunderstandings vanished. We know just where we went wrong.'

'I think,' Stone replied quietly, 'that we all of us know now where we went wrong. For myself I am completely satisfied in that I have achieved my life's ambition. For just one precious moment I was able to gaze upon the face of the Ultimate. It satisfied me that all I ever believed was correct.'

'Then you saw what we saw?' Edna asked quickly. 'A kind of radiant shaft of light from above — ?'

'I saw much more than that,' Jonathan Stone replied gravely.

'We saw something like a ray of light.' Lucille put in. 'I mean Martin and I — but it meant a great deal more to Mr. Stone. He's capable of seeing much further than that.'

'And did anything happen to you because of what you saw?' Edna asked quickly — at which Martin Senior nodded slowly.

'There was a strange shifting of

viewpoint. Somehow everything mental became abruptly crystal clear — like looking into oneself, and the effect hasn't gone off either. I saw, for the briefest instant, how futile a thing murder is.'

'Murder?' Jerry repeated, astonished.

'That startles you, eh? Well, let me tell you that up to that moment of conversion I had murder in my heart. I brought it with me from Earth. Just before we were whisked away I had planned, quite cunningly I thought, the murder of a young woman who was once a friend of mine. Frustration and a nurtured desire for vengeance had made of me a bitter, hard-lipped man. Now all that has evaporated. Not only do I clearly see the senselessness of murder, but I even turn from it with revulsion. One might put it all down to a purifying effect, I suppose?'

'Or to swift evolution,' Edna mused, 'Where formerly I had no scientific knowledge whatever I now have it in excelsis. I can even contemplate the infinite calculus and see the answer without the least effort. That can only be explained by a swift and profound mental advancement — and advancement is evolution.'

'That's it!' Jerry snapped his fingers. 'Each one of us has evolved to a point which humanity, under normal circumstances, would probably only reach in millions of years. Cosmic rays have done it — and are still doing it. As our minds have advanced and improved so have our bodies because the physical always obeys the mental. In one stroke, in a few hours of Earth-time, we have telescoped millions of years of advancement.'

'And may yet go further,' Lucille said quietly. 'For me there has not come so much mental change as physical release from the disease which was killing me. I have nobody present who can positively say that I am cured: I just know that I am.'

'If you know it,' Stone said, 'it doesn't matter what anybody else thinks. You are your own mistress, Lucille, as long as you retain an individuality.'

The silence weighed heavy for a while. The assimilation of the fact that each one of them had become a genius, and that this state of rarefied intellectual eminence was still developing, was slow indeed. Earth-born habits and inhibitions were not that easy to cast aside. Each had been born of a human being and they had yet to outgrow the tenacious roots of heredity.

'How far do you suppose we can develop before reaching maximum?' Jerry asked abruptly — and as usual he directed the question to the venerable Jonathan Stone.

'Maximum,' Stone answered, 'is purely an arbitrary term set by human beings to denote a period beyond which they cannot predict anything certain. I would say that development is unbounded, infinite, free and — '

It was mid-evening. In the distance a brass band was playing on the barmy air. Children were laughing and gambolling some distance away. Jerry, instead of getting the complete answer to his question, found himself near the pavilion counter. Edna was standing close beside him. They looked at each other in profound bewilderment — and then around them. The rationed foods they had set out had vanished: they were back on their shelves. There was no sign of Jonathan Stone, Lucille, or Martin Senior.

'What's — happened?' Jerry demanded, his eyes blank. 'Or did I dream something?'

'It was no dream,' Edna reassured him, and those few words convinced him that he was not going insane. 'Look at our sunburn! Just as it was when we were . . . '

Baffled, they raced to the pavilion doorway. Everything was perfectly normal. Ahead of them lay a stretch of grassy earth, with two trees — just as they had been in that alien space. Under one of them, on a rustic seat, sat an elderly white-haired man looking at a small Bible. Near him a shapely girl with golden-brown skin lay coiled on the grass. Further away still a young man sat against the second tree and looked about him. Beyond this immediate area children tumbled, giggled, and turned head-over-heels.

'I don't get it,' Jerry whispered, his hand on Edna's arm. 'Look at the clock over there!'

Edna looked, and started. It was just after 9.15 — only the merest fraction, and even that time could have been occupied in moving to the doorway and contemplating the scenery.

'My watch also says nine-fifteen,' Jerry whispered. 'Last time I looked at it, it was heading for three o'clock!'

'Those children were just outside the slice which went elsewhere,' Edna said, almost irrelevantly.

'It didn't happen!' Jerry insisted stubbornly. 'It couldn't! Nothing's different and no time has elapsed. We had bad dreams — or good ones. Damned if I know which.'

'Could you feel as you do towards me, and could I feel as I do towards you, merely on the strength of a dream?' Edna asked quietly. 'That's something very real, Jerry, and very lovely. We no longer have the towering genius, but the character change in each of us remains.'

'It seems so . . . ' Jerry's admission was made with a frown of complete bewilderment, then his grip on Edna's arm tightened a little as Jonathan Stone,

Lucille, and Martin Senior all began to move at the same instant. They glanced towards each other, rose from their various positions, and converged into a trio.

'That proves it did happen!' Jerry insisted. 'Before the incident in alien space they didn't even know each other: now they meet like old friends.'

The three came forward. In the eyes of Martin Senior and Lucille there was utter bafflement, but Jonathan Stone seemed to be smiling. And the vigorous uprightness which had come to him Elsewhere was still there. So, too, with the young man and woman the evidences were proclaimed by the bronze of their skin and the easy grace of their movements.

'Apparently,' Jonathan Stone said, pocketing his Bible, 'we are back!'

'But it happened!' Lucille insisted. 'I'm absolutely sure that it happened! I know it did because I feel so well, so happy, so sure of myself and the future.'

'And I know it happened because I no longer have murder in my heart,' Martin Senior added. 'But when did it happen? See that clock over there? It's still only a few minutes after nine-fifteen! According to that we never went at all.'

'We went — and we came back,' Jonathan Stone said, shrugging. 'Whilst we were there we lost nearly all our human failings and weaknesses, and I had my unforgettable experience of seeing the Ultimate face to face. But, though the physical changes remain the genius of speeding evolution has gone like mist.'

'Why?' Edna insisted.

'Because we are again surrounded by multi-millions of conflicting minds all unconsciously influencing our efforts to think straight. That means the evaporation of that brief genius, but it does not mean a step backwards to the former mental and physical state. Those conditions were destroyed forever and the correct adjustment made, not so much by the cosmic rays themselves as by the touch of the Artisan of the Universe himself.'

'Yes, but — ' Edna moved restlessly. 'Mr. Stone, it still does not explain why it happened! We did so much, have brought back such incredible changes, and yet no time elapsed!'

'Time,' Stone smiled, 'is only a unit of measurement used by human beings to bring order into what would otherwise appear as chaos. In any case that experience was not Earthly, or even mundane, so how could Time as we know it be applied to it? Time is not absolute, you know. There is a flaw in it. Where, for instance, is the moment between present and future? You may say the next second is in the future, but the instant you say it, it is in the present, and before you realize it, it is in the past! What is in the tiny, infinitesimal gap between? No matter to what inconceivably small unit you reduce Time-instants, you can never find the bridge between this instant and the next. Maybe we did bridge it for a moment.'

'There must have been a reason,' Jerry insisted; then suddenly raising his voice he called over to him the children who were rioting nearby. They came immediately — dusty, happy, hot-faced girls and boys, their clothes in a condition that would probably give their mothers a fit when they arrived home.

'You kids been here for the last

half-hour?' Jerry asked.

'Bin here all evening!'

'Time we went home, too!' One of the girls looked startled. 'It's twenty-past nine!'

'Whilst you were playing about did you see anything queer happen?' Jerry insisted.

'Queer, mister? How'd y'mean? Queer?'

'Well, for instance, was there an earth-quake or some sort? A loud explosion? Did this pavilion here vanish?'

The blank stares were enough; then a boy with freckles and a sawn-off nose made a rude face.

'You've bin out in the sun too long, mister! Come on, gang: time we got 'ome . . . '

'Satisfied?' Jonathan Stone asked dryly, and Jerry shook his head.

'I'll never be that. I'll go through the rest of my life wondering what caused our experience to happen.'

'So will all of us probably.' Martin Senior shrugged. 'For myself I'm pre-pared to accept it for what it was — just one of those things.'

'For which,' Lucille muttered, 'we

should be unspeakably grateful. As to the reason for it: evidently there isn't one.'

★　★　★

But of course she was wrong in this. The reason was nakedly plain, but such is the inscrutability of things Professor Engleman had not the least idea of having precipitated anything unusual. He stood now beside the switch of his disturber-field machine and contemplated it. Then he shook his head slowly.

'I have the feeling, ladies and gentlemen, that it might not be altogether safe to operate this machine this evening,' he said. 'I have just switched on and off — a matter of a split second — and I distinctly noticed a curious stress in the air, a kind of warping of forces. Now that should not be, particularly as I might miss our intended target of St. Michael's statue. It is possible the instrument has been thrown out of alignment in its removal to this hall.'

'Surely you can risk it?' one of the scientists asked, quite disappointed.

'Risk it? Great heavens, no! You do not realize the power of this instrument, my dear sir. Not power, as such, but the power to cause a shift in the probability of matter itself! Unless I am absolutely sure of my target I dare not set the machine at work. You see, the field of disturbance set up, unless absolutely exact, might cause the electron-probabilities of any number of people or objects to suddenly yield to the probability that they are somewhere else. The whole thing is utterly unpredictable. In a single instant any part of the universe might change places with another part — such is the Law of Probability.'

'Supposing,' another scientist asked, 'such a thing did really happen. Would the transposition be absolute? Permanent?'

'No, not necessarily,' Engleman replied, after some thought. 'Everything in the Universe has its proper place, and remains there unless interfered with by an outside source. My disturber-field is such an outside source. As long as it operated it would transpose a part of the Universe, but the moment the disturbance was cut off the normal process would instantly return, just as an elastic snaps back to its original length when tension ceases.'

'During which time immense damage might be done!' another scientist protested.

'Damage?' Engleman raised his eyebrows. 'Why no, my friend. The disturber-field operates in what I call hyper-Time, which is a complex way of saying it operates between the normal instants of Time. Since it is apart from the normal order of the Universe it cannot operate within the normal Time-span. Yes,' Engleman sighed, 'very unpredictable, and I am sorry not to be able to give you a demonstration. Indeed, perhaps I should work out the details much more carefully before I make any experiments. I'm glad I had the presence of mind to switch off my machine a second after I switched on. Had I continued, anything might have happened. As it is, all is well. At a later date I will call you all together again to witness something of real interest . . . '

Which brought the meeting to a close

and left Engleman perfectly satisfied that, so far, he had not transgressed any laws of Nature. Five people at that moment walking thoughtfully from the Great Park could have told him a very different story.

3

Yithan Kan

My name is Amos Latham, and I am, I hope, a reasonably intelligent man. I know nearly all the subjects encompassed in a modern education, but I must admit my knowledge fell far short on the day that I found an object resembling the half shell of a walnut lying at the bottom of a neatly drilled five-foot hole in my best sweet pea bed.

My job? In a way, I'm a farmer. I like to experiment in grafting, pursue if possible hybrid experiments on the lines laid down by Mendel.

I found the walnut on June 7th, just six days ago. It was a perplexing puzzle in itself to decide how an object so small, unless it were a meteorite, had got to such a depth overnight — but the puzzle deepened when I found that by no means at hand could I begin to budge it!

I began to suspect the thing had some sort of under part that went down like a shaft into the ground at the bottom of the hole it had burrowed — that what I saw was only the upper part of some sort of buried spear. That being so, the only thing to do was to clear the sides of the thin shaft and dig the object out.

It took me half a day to make the shaft wide enough to permit me getting down it, but even then I was no better off. I could see clearly enough that the walnut was simply a hemisphere of shell-like substance — but of a vastly incredible weight! I strained and tugged at it until my fingers ached. But I couldn't shift it in the slightest. I just couldn't convince myself that such a fact was true — but it was.

To say my curiosity was aroused is putting it mildly. I went into the garage and brought out a block and tackle. I erected it on a pretty stout scaffolding tripod and fixed the chain clamp around the inch-square lump. The tripod snapped, but the object didn't budge!

That settled it. Beyond question I'd

happened on something that was outside all normal laws, at least in the matter of weight. I remembered something about electrons and protons in contact — neutrons — and went inside the house to telephone Bradley.

Bradley is a physicist, in the employ of the Bureau of Standards. He arrived late that afternoon. Bradley, with his usual foresight, had brought along a powerful breakdown truck, complete with crane, trailing behind his car.

I greeted him warmly as he came toward the house, but as he returned the greeting there was a doubt in his closely set grey eyes.

'Where is this walnut of yours?' he asked, after we had had a drink. I took him out to the sweet pea bed, or rather what was left of it after my excavation work.

The thing was still there, and the faint smile vanished from Bradley's face as he tried vainly to shift it.

'Boy, you have got onto something!' he whistled in amazement. 'If that stuff belongs on this world I'm clean crazy.

Anyway, we'll soon see.'

Scrambling back to the top of the small crater he signalled the truck-men. They backed their conveyance clumsily into the garden and watched curiously as they lowered the crane chain. Finally we managed to encompass the walnut in the clamp and gave the pull away order.

A terrific strain was thrown on the chain as it slowly creaked and groaned over the winch. Powerful though the truck's engine was it took every vestige of it to lift that absurdly tiny thing from the ground. Very slowly it rose up, inch by inch. We saw that the underside was apparently like the rest of it. Brad was watching the thing keenly.

Finally, we had the object deposited on a huge stone block that had once been part of a well at the bottom of the garden. There the task of the astounded truckers ended. They went off round-eyed and puzzled in a settling haze of dust, leaving us both to our own devices.

Smoking pensively, Bradley studied the object for a while, then turned to me.

'Dense as hell,' he said bluntly. 'Pretty

similar to the stuff that must exist at the core of Earth, though infinitely denser than even that.' I nodded slowly and waited for him to continue.

'That lump came from somewhere out in space,' he resumed. 'Where, we don't know, but we can hazard a guess — probably from the region of the giant star areas. Specks of substance like this floating around in space probably made up the cores of the very worlds around us — stuff so densely packed that it had an unbelievable weight. It may be a fragment from a sun where matter is densely packed.'

'You mean a white dwarf?' I suggested.

He nodded.

'That's it. Take the Companion of Sirius, for example. That is a white dwarf, and Adams at Mount Wilson Observatory proved long ago that the density there is two thousand times greater than that of platinum. Take a matchbox full of the stuff and it would require a derrick to raise it. That's the kind of thing we've got here. That's why it ploughed so deep into the earth when it arrived. Strange it didn't burn up; can't quite figure out that angle.'

I pondered. Physics isn't entirely in my line; but Brad hadn't finished talking. He studied the object more closely for a while, then went on.

'Come to think of it, this substance might not be from a sun, but from a cooled world. Eddington told us that heat is not entirely necessary for compressibility of matter. It is not essential to have a temperature of about ten million degrees in order to smash atoms. Terrific pressure alone will suffice.

'The shell of satellite electrons which can be broken by the attacks of X-rays, or the fierce collisions going on in the interior of a star, can also break by the application of continued pressure on a dense world. This produces an almost bare nucleus with the heavier atoms retaining a few of the closest electrons, forming a structure of perhaps one hundredth of a complete atom.

'The consequent compression produces vast weight by comparison with sizes to which we're accustomed. Take the example in physics: in a monatomic gas like helium a thirty-two fold increase in pressure gives an eight fold increase of density, if the heat of compression is retained in the gas. There you have an example of heat pressure — but on a world that is a child of a compressed sun — the Companion of Sirius for example — the very pressure of that world would produce similar, even far greater results. At the very roughest estimate this thing here weighs about one ton to the cubic inch — and that's plenty heavy!'

'And now that it's here what do we do with it?' I asked quietly.

He shrugged.

'Nothing we can do, except give it to the meteorite section of the museum. I'll make arrangements for it to be picked up. It'll be about two weeks, though; I've a special Government job waiting for me.'

Talking, we went into the house and had dinner. It was late when Brad finally left with the promise to return in two weeks. Once I'd seen him off I strolled over in the moonlight calm to survey again that uncanny lump.

But it had changed! I got quite a shock as the rays of the amber moon smote now upon a tiny, tortoise-like head. Bent legs, exceptionally powerful, jutted outward from the shell. The legs moved slowly as I went toward the thing, but it stopped on the stone. Perhaps it realized that to fall off would mean another five-foot plunge into the ground.

I studied the creature from a distance, observing the viciously curved scar of a mouth. Its resemblance to a tortoise was now quite remarkable. It was smaller, of course, and incredibly heavier!

I shall never know if it was impulse or plain curiosity that prompted me to extend an ingratiating hand toward it. Not knowing what type of intelligence the thing possessed that seemed the only way I could show friendship.

A second later I regretted it. The tiny head shot forward toward my outstretched hand, faster than the striking paw of a cat. Before I knew it the creature's terrible mouth had scissored open and shut. There was a momentary gleam of small, needle-pointed teeth.

Then I was gazing at a numbed, crimsoned finger from which the top, to the first knuckle, had been completely severed!

For a second or two I hardly knew what to think, the shock stunned me. I blundered back into the house, cauterized and bandaged the numbed member. Then, fuming with anger both at the hostility of my visitor and my own stupidity, I sat down to figure the thing out.

I didn't get very far. I couldn't understand how a thing like the walnut had travelled through the void of space and arrived with an impact that had buried it five feet in the ground — yet could live here in an atmosphere of oxygen and hydrogen. Either it was completely adaptable to both space and air, or else it had travelled in some kind of protecting case that had fallen away at the frictional heat of our upper atmosphere.

I meditated once upon killing the infernal thing, but I refrained for two reasons. The bullet would probably glance off such armour-plated density. Secondly, the object was going to interest the scientists. I made up my mind to call Bradley the next day.

My sleep was strangely disturbed — physically by the burning pain of returning sensation in my injured finger, and mentally by the memory of the walnut and the realization in my occasional wakeful spells that it was still outside, a densely heavy, vicious-jawed devil.

At times I dreamed, but they were dreams of a quality surely denied to any sane man. I beheld a world of intense darkness lying still and airless under a sky powdered with unfamiliar nebulae and constellations. There was a sense of vast loneliness and incompleteness, of enormous stretches of time occupied by an abstract state that I could only roughly determine as meditation. Meditation? By the walnut? Well, that was how it looked.

As though to substantiate my guess I glimpsed the walnut upon this darkly empty plain, surrounded by the outlines of what dimly appeared to be a city — but a city with no earthly similarity, ruled by

135

machines and yet deserted. In the midst of these perplexing immensities the walnut brooded alone —

Suddenly I was awake, feverishly hot, with a name burning in my brain, the oddest, most astounding name. It sounded like —Yithan Kan. I screamed it out three times, then suddenly remembered where I was. Dazedly I looked through the window toward the dawn light. That ton weight dark object was still on the block of stone. I shuddered. The memory of that ghastly dream with its terrific sense of weight and loneliness was still seared into my mind.

I felt ill as I got up and dressed. My finger had ceased bleeding but was anything but healthy to look at. It had taken on a curious brittle appearance most unusual for normal coagulation. The finger itself felt curiously different — leaden is the only way to describe it.

I thought once of phoning Doc Shaw to come over. Then, mainly because I detest the fussiness of physicians and because of my complete faith in my own first aid efforts I let the idea drop. Instead I phoned New York, but to my annoyance

Bradley was already in Washington. It occurred to me with a sudden panicky feeling that for another two weeks I would be alone with this atrocity from an unknown world — unless of course I took the obvious course and left.

I decided against that. Don't ask me why: I can only put it down to the same lure that drives perfectly sane men into absolute danger by the very force of some intangible fascination. I went outside and watched the walnut in the hot morning sunshine. Its capacity for motionlessness amazed me. It did not seem to have budged a thirty-second of an inch since it had been placed there.

Keeping a respectable distance away I decided to call out that absurd name.

'Yithan Kan! Yithan Kan,' I shouted, 'can you hear me? Can you understand me?'

The beady eyes, like microscopic garnets, studied me unwaveringly, and I returned the stare like a man hypnotized by a snake. That very act did something to me. I could feel a groping and plucking at the neurons and receptive cells of my brain.

That which followed was not exactly an exchange of communications — in fact I do not believe my brain was developed enough to pass any coherent thought. It was more a series of mental images from which I gathered that this weird object, on arrival, had been stunned by the terrific impact. Only its super hardness and density had saved its life.

It was, as I had guessed, perfectly adaptable to any conditions. Its natural environment was one of intense cold — interstellar cold. Here on Earth it had apparently adapted itself immediately to the drastic change in conditions. I have heard of plants with such amazing adaptability, but the idea of an intelligent organism with similar abilities was unbelievable. Much to my surprise I learned that Yithan Kan was the female of its species.

So much I gathered on that first communication, then the spell was broken by some slight sound made by the wind. Disturbed in both mind and body I went into the house and tried to figure out what I ought to do, particularly how to improve my physical condition. I felt bone weary, and for no apparent reason.

It occurred to me that I might have been poisoned by the bite, but a second examination of my injured finger and a study of a droplet of blood through my microscope revealed no such signs. I wasn't poisoned; it was something else that had gripped me — something subtly different.

Several times I wondered if I ought to feed the walnut, then decided it didn't seem necessary. From what I could gather it absorbed energy directly — probably from the shorter cosmic rays that abound freely in space and also to a good extent on Earth.

With the passage of time my conviction of illness increased. From my injured finger the leaden sensation had travelled the entire length of my arm, changing it from normal colour to a stone gray hue. I began to become really alarmed.

As I prepared lunch, though I did it more from force of habit than because I was hungry, I received another shock. I'd decided on canned beans to go with some cold meat, and in the most natural fashion possible I grabbed the tin with my injured hand to pull it from the shelf.

The can felt like pulp in my grasp — I found myself staring in amazement as juice and squashed beans spurted from the cracks in the tin, so tightly had I gripped it! I doubt if a hammer could have flattened it more effectively. I dropped the battered can in stupefied horror then looked at my hand. It wasn't scarred or cut by the can's sharp edges — only weighted, almost without feeling, horribly numb. I flexed my fingers that I could hardly feel — all save the injured one that wouldn't move at all.

I forgot all about a meal; the complexity of this new happening forced me to start pacing around, trying to figure out what had occurred.

From a sense of horror I graduated by easy stages to one of interest, even triumph. I spent some time testing my strength on the hardest things I could find, felt a certain joy in discovering that most metals would bend easily in my one-handed grip, that even small stones crushed into powder as though cramped in a vice.

Of course, I knew that the walnut was at the bottom of it. But how had this thing come about? Had the bite it had given me started some condition of matter such as could only exist on the unknown, unimaginably heavy world from which the creature had come? What was the explanation?

Man, clearly, is what the scientists vaguely call a 'fortuitous concourse of atoms in the shape of a man,' a concourse that has the mystic power of thinking. He is in effect a very definite movable knot of energy condensed into a visible form. In the beginning of time some cosmic radiation changed a free energy state into a definite material build-up called protoplasm, and after the intermediate stages it became Man.

Somewhere, the enigmatic occurrence of mutations had come about — the definite change from one species into another effected by — Just what? Science is still hazy on that. Maybe radiations once again — unseen, undetectable, operating upon material structures at certain intervals of time.

These radiations have produced through the ages a change so enormous as to elevate protoplasm into living man. Nothing has been destroyed because nothing in the universe *can* be destroyed: only change is possible. Unseen forces altered atoms into a new concourse, formed a new pattern, and ultimately built them into the shape of Man.

But if this entity possessed — as was highly probable — many of these spatial radiations as part of its natural make-up, it was also possible that in the fashion of radium's hideously destructive emanations, a good deal of radiation had entered my body at the moment of that finger severance. And, since this creature was infinitely more powerful than I, representing a far mightier state of condensed matter, it would be possible to bend me entirely to its own matter state just as a strong will can over-power a weak one.

In that case the atoms and electrons of my body were even now undergoing a change! Pressures and radiations, operating on an infinitely small scale, were at work within me, changing my whole natural formation into a new condition of matter!

My strength! The dead weight increasing in my arm! The crawling numbness creeping around my shoulders and neck!

'God!' I cried hoarsely, leaping up as the searing truth struck home to me. 'God — ' I brought my hand down bitterly on the table with the intensity of my thoughts. The tabletop splintered as though split with an axe.

I scarcely heeded it. I had become accustomed by now to the frightful power of that left arm. With every hour it was growing heavier, tauter, more unwieldy — yet as the same conviction of strain passed around my shoulders I began to feel an awareness of new balance. I felt less one-sided. It could only mean that my new weight was distributing itself equally by slow degrees.

Struck with a sudden thought I hunted up a tape line and, standing flat against a wall, measured myself. I felt a queer sensation at my heart when I discovered I was two inches shorter in height! Then a compressing, contracting effect was in force! My mass was becoming smaller and denser.

Frightened, I went outside and tried to communicate with the walnut, but my brain emanations were useless. Nor did the thing attempt to communicate with me, though it watched me with motionless intentness.

But the reason for it all? That was what I could not understand. That bite had been deliberate; the walnut had purposely impregnated me. But to what purpose? Sheer malice? No; any intelligence so profound would not stoop to so earthly a thing as malice. There was another reason — perhaps it lay somewhere in the realms of those weird, disturbing dreams I had had.

And still no thought of leaving entered my head, or if it did I refused to heed it. I believe the creature itself was responsible for that, holding me by some Indefinable shackle of will power, forcing me onward into a state I could only guess at, but which savoured with every passing hour of a place unworldly, lying across inconceivable distances.

Quite suddenly, toward evening, the sickly feeling that had persisted with me all day passed off. I became ravenously hungry. I had an appetite that would have done credit to a lumberjack.

In the space of an hour I had emptied my small but well stocked refrigerator, but even then I only felt vaguely satisfied. I knew that it would not be long before I would have to eat again.

Energy, of course — strange, mysterious changes within me that demanded a sudden terrific influx of supply to keep pace with my rate of increasing strength. Very similar, I decided, to the tautness of a spring governing the exact amount of potential energy it must possess.

By the time I went to bed — after a final dubious look at the motionless walnut in the rising moonlight — I was feeling very top heavy indeed. The effect seemed to be working downward from my arms and shoulder — for my other arm was now likewise affected to the lower extremities.

The bed creaked noisily as I lay upon it. I was asleep almost immediately and once again strange, incredible dreams penetrated my mind. But this time my brain was much clearer, remarkably sharpened. I saw the things that were offered to me by some kind of extra sensory reception. Records of a strange race buried in a long-lost antiquity on a world of huge weight, were laid bare before me.

I saw again that dark, unfriendly airless world with its vaulted dome of unfamiliar stars. This time I saw others of the Walnut race — spawning thousands. Through flickering, kaleidoscopic flashes I watched a strange disease, apparently an unfavourable radiation from outer space, attack one after another of the beings, wipe them out with the efficiency that lethal gas kills a man.

I realized more clearly than ever that these beings did sustain themselves by radiations. To them, a sudden influx of abnormal radiation was a perfect cosmic Black Plague, absolutely fatal in effect. I saw the death of thousands upon thousands of the creatures until there could not have been more than five remaining.

Here the disease stopped, but four of

the five died slowly from after-effects, leaving only one — Yithan Kan!

One, a female of the species, surrounded by the glory of a magnificently intelligent race's discoveries, yet unable alone to do anything with them. Unable to mate, unable to perpetuate the superb science of her species.

She seemed to meditate over the perplexity of this problem for years. I saw her study machines that had no earthly meaning. Telescopes of surpassing power revealed to her the unrevealed depths of the cosmos on polished mirrors of floating mercury. The dead worlds of Sirius, the half-formed worlds of Arcturus, the rich but lifeless worlds whirling around vast Antares and Betelgeuse — these she studied, without avail.

Then the instruments' powers reached out across immeasurable light years to the regions of the dwarf G-type suns, to the Solar System. Mercury, Venus, Mars, and the outer planets were mirrored perfectly in the instruments, but Yithan Kan found no traces of life in any of them. That seemed to be the treasured possession of the third world alone.

Yithan Kan seemed to come to a decision. Her head and legs folded inside her shell-like body. She generated gravity neutralization as simply as a spider spins its web, and hurtled bullet-like into the swirling, dusty emptiness overhead.

I awoke suddenly with visions of galaxies, suns and planets whirling before my vision. It was morning, and I was no longer in bed. No! The bed had collapsed under my weight in the night, precipitating me onto a floor that was showing signs of cracking.

My heaviness now was a terrific burden. During the night I had changed incredibly, was literally half my previous size with an energy and strength beyond belief.

Hunger, terror, wonderment — these three things battled in my mind as I lumbered creakingly across the cracking floor. I gained the doorway safely enough, but I fell through the staircase and landed in the kitchen below! I wasn't hurt. No indeed! Where I had struck myself against the woodwork it had splintered and left my hardened, stone-gray flesh untouched!

I went into the yard, strangled a dozen chickens one after the other and ate them raw. I was no longer Amos Latham; I was something metamorphosing into an unknown state for an equally unknown purpose. I knew now how Yithan Kan had come to Earth, but the *why* still defeated me.

I knew, too, that if she wanted she could easily get off that stone block without dropping to the ground. Her natural power of gravity neutralization would accomplish that. Only when she had been unconscious from her great fall had she weighed her normal ton to the cubic inch.

Her wine-red little eyes watched me as I ravenously ate the fowls. I didn't try to communicate: I had all my work cut out to master my own movements and control my will power. Going back into the house I thought of the idea of recording my experiences, and up to now I think I have managed to maintain a certain coherency.

It is not easy to write this because I have to have my hand fastened to a rope slung to a beam in the garage roof so that the weight of my arm and hand does not interfere with writing. If this writing is thick and heavy it is because I am constantly wearing down the pencil point, frequently breaking the pencils themselves. The very lightest of pressure suffices.

I feel now that I may revert to the present tense because I have caught up with my experiments to date. There is nothing for me now but to state events as they happen, and I have the oddest conception that they will happen soon.

⋆ ⋆ ⋆

I have been resting. At least I call it that for want of a better term. In truth, it was more a comatose condition occasioned, I think, by exhaustion. The vast change in my makeup, the enigmatic forcing together of electronic spaces by unknown radiations, the consequent denser packing of materials by scientific powers that I can hardly guess at, tires me with amazing rapidity. But during that sleep, if sleep it was, I dreamed again.

Yithan Kan is more than a mere scientist. She has the knowledge of a brilliant race at her command. The forces of light, space, gravitation and pressure are solved riddles to her mind. I have learned that my earlier hypothesis — that a matter formation can be altered by radiation into what is possibly a new and unthought of state — is correct. By radiations from her own body she has mastered mine, literally is bending its formation to conform with her wishes.

I have eaten again, and now I feel that that huge hunger is abating, maybe by the establishment of some new level of change. I am smaller, infinitely smaller, yet the mass of my body is infinitely increased, compressed to an unbelievable weight.

I no longer dare to go inside the house. Floors and furniture splinter under my weight . . . I have substituted a chain for a rope to support the pencil, but live in fear that the beam, a foot thick though it is, will smash in two if I do not stop writing . . . Yet I must go on.

I think I have been unconscious again — it seems to me that days have drifted by. Perhaps it s a good thing that I am so far from town; people rarely pass around here. With my last awakening I became conscious of a new sense, which still persists.

I can sense the inflow of cosmic radiations, such as are quite undetectable to normal human beings. They give me life, strength, an abounding energy that is both glorious and yet oddly terrifying.

Around me is a world of giantism. The garage seems to me like a vast hall; this very pencil is far bigger than I. I am forced to work it like a lever — but now it is simpler because I have taken on a neutralizing power. The radiations I absorb from space I can convert within myself to neutralizing uses.

You wonder? Why should you? A plant breaks down nitrogen; a human being inhales oxygen and hydrogen and exhales, by the use of inner chemistry, carbon dioxide. Is it so wonderful that I absorb energies and transmit them in their most-needed form — for the nullification of weight? No, it is not impossible but — I forget! I am no longer human, therefore I no longer think properly along human lines.

Do not ask me to explain the full state of my metamorphosis; I have tried to do that already, to tell by the stages through which it happened how Yithan Kan reassembled my bodily atoms so completely as to give me a body no more than an inch in diameter, yet weighing very nearly a ton, without neutralization.

All this she has accomplished without causing death, as easily indeed as in my own experiments I have grafted cuttings from one tree onto another without killing either. Organic life is truly indeed simply an arrangement — in the higher states — of living, thinking matter that, by a mind clever enough, can be altered into a new and entirely unpredictable state.

From this doorway I can see Yithan Kan very clearly. She is as big as I, high atop a mighty block of stone — a stone that was only an ordinary block on the day that she was first put there. I am like a microscopic tortoise, hardly visible. I am no longer an Earth being, for I am not breathing — only absorbing radiations. The entity of Amos Latham has gone and instead I am — *what*?

At last I grasp the purpose of Yithan Kan's visit. I can feel her mental radiations coming to me, and with those radiations the faint leftover human traces of my mind evince a certain admiration for the nobility, the ruthless purpose of her aim.

For the perpetuation of her race and science she needs a mate — a male. I am still a male. She metamorphosed me into a being identical wither herself save in the matter of sex — as easily as a sculptor can model a piece of clay into a woman and then into a dog without changing the clay. He merely reforms the atoms and molecules of the clay into a new shape.

And what does he use for his tools? Basically, force! In like manner, but fully understanding the absolute nature of the force *behind* force, Yithan Kan has remoulded me.

She needs me . . . and I need her! I know I do. I feel it. She is compelling to me now — fascinating. Our children on that far distant world beyond Sirius will carry on the heritage of a race entirely eliminated excepted for this indomitable one — Yithan Kan. Afterward, the nucleus of a new race. A reaching upward toward achievement.

I must go to Yithan Kan. Earth no longer holds me. At will I can, and shall, leave it behind — wing across the cosmos with Yithan Kan to her distant planet.

I shall go. I must go. Now!

4

He Never Slept

My own particular participation in that which follows is slight. Merely for the purpose of verification, should you desire it, I state that my name is Richard Finsbury, and that I am a Londoner born and bred. At any time you may reach me at the Royal College Hospital, London.

I am, in truth, merely the chronicler of a diary, left solely to my discretion by Dr. Jason Veldor, the renowned psychologist, and perhaps at one time the most sought-after man on mental troubles that ever graced the grey confines of London.

His diary presents a tale as bizarre and extraordinary as any I have yet encountered, but as I personally knew Dr. Veldor extremely well, had witnessed practically all his experiments, and knew him for what he was — an iron-willed, courageous, upright man — I do not for one moment dare to presume that he wrote a single word of falsehood. First let me relate the few events that led up to the final passing into my hands of his amazing diary.

It was, as I remember, a bleak and miserable day in November when an urgent letter reached me at the College Hospital. It was from Veldor himself, whom I had seen only at infrequent intervals since I had studied medicine under him, and was, I think, his favourite pupil. Without hesitation, my work at that time not being of an exacting nature, I went to his home in Kensington. I remember, as I looked at the worn steps, thinking how many times I had gone up and down them in my days of study.

Walmsley, the manservant, let me in, and in a moment I was in Dr. Veldor's cosy study, and gazing once more on that pleasant but compelling face.

He was almost bald and possessed a remarkably high forehead, while beneath it were his unforgettable, dark-blue, almost hypnotic eyes, magnified slightly by large, gold-rimmed glasses. The

157

hooked, eagle-like nose, downwardly curved thin mouth, and out-jutting un-dimpled chin, all betokened the man of dogmatism and great will power. I never once angered the doctor, nor do I think it would have been a very safe procedure to do so.

'Ah, Richard,' he said, using as always my Christian name, 'I hope you will forgive me for upsetting your work with my letter, but really I have discovered something extremely interesting; indeed, I ventured to think quite unheard-of as yet in the annals of science.' He waved me to a chair and went on with hardly a pause. 'You know, Richard, I have always looked upon you as something very close to a son. Your views and ideals are very closely allied to mine. You know that?' His big, magnetic eyes looked into mine.

'Of course, sir,' I answered, helping myself to a cigarette from the box he pushed across the paper-littered desk. 'Everything you do is of the greatest interest to me. After all, not every young medical student in London can call the great Dr. Veldor his friend.'

He laughed slightly. 'Forget my fame, Richard — forget everything save the fact that I am going to talk to you as man to man. I have great faith in you, my boy — faith that one day you will take up scientific medicine where I leave it off. It is because I may leave off a trifle sooner than is normal that I have sent for you.'

I started at that. 'But, sir, you don't mean that — '

He waved me into silence with a big, powerful hand. 'I am going to undertake an experiment that may endanger my life, Richard. I am going to make an experiment which, if successful, will mean in the future a healthier and far less frightened humanity.'

'But if the experiment is so inimical to life, why can't you find somebody else to experiment on?' I asked anxiously. 'Somebody who is not famous, who is not so much needed as you are.'

The powerful chin expanded in width as he smiled grimly. 'I am not afraid to do to myself what I would do to others,' he replied gravely, and looked at me solemnly for a space. Then, alert again: 'Besides, I doubt if anybody else would be able to do what I have in mind. In case anything should happen to me, Richard, you will take sole possession of this diary here' — he laid his hand on a thick black volume at his elbow — 'and the remainder of my scientific apparatus, money, et cetera, will be disposed of according to my will. You understand that?'

'Quite, sir, but I don't like the way you're talking. I don't want to lose you!'

'You may not,' he answered slowly. 'I can't be sure,' and I silently marvelled at the cool way he deliberated his chances of surviving death. 'In any case, sacrifice is always the keynote of scientific progress. To come to my point, Richard, I have for many years been very disgusted with the fact that all the human race — indeed every living organism — must waste a third of its life in sleep. Think what a race we'd be if we never slept!' His big eyes glowed strangely as he uttered the words.

I pondered on that. Certainly it was an unusual idea.

'Sleep and dreams are closely allied,' he

went on, clasping his hands and looking at me broodingly. 'We waste half our lives because we cannot control the dreams of our sleeping selves; we do not understand what use to put them to. There is a something beyond sleep, Richard, that I am going to unearth. I am going to explore a dream!'

'That sounds like a fairy tale, sir,' I ventured.

But he shook his great head. 'Not a fairy tale, Richard — scientific fact. My aim is to find a way to end the need of sleep and to determine thoroughly what happens during the period when the brain or the will no longer controls the movements of the body. I do not believe, like Freud, that dreams are suppressed desires, nor do I altogether concur with the views of Fortnum-Roscoe. It is my own belief that dreams are the experiences of another character, allied maybe by some other dimension, with one's own three-dimensional consciousness. At will, or sometimes unbidden, these dream states — this other unknown self — controls the consciousness.

'Robert Louis Stevenson, the famous author, if you recollect, used to place himself in a condition of self-suggestion before he went to sleep. The resultant effects, dreams, were so vivid that many times they provided sequences in his books. You will find that fact in his book 'Across the Plains', Richard, if you are ever minded to read it. Very interesting. In other instances we have dreams occasioned by pure hypnotism, which are always more vivid than those of a more normal nature.

'Again, it seems to be the memory furthest from our waking thoughts, the one with the seemingly greatest gap from the mundane, that is the most vivid. That is a mystery that interests me, Richard. Always, though, there is some reason for a dream — some of the reasons quite natural, but others entirely unexplained. Whence come these sleep figments? And why should it be necessary to sleep in order to bring them into being?

'I am confident that they are but the manifestations of some other self, a self that is a real entity and yet untouchable from our waking dimension. An entity that exists in our waking hours in the guise of something subconscious — by which we might explain such things as sixth sense, intuition, and so forth — and in sleep as a dream. Richard, I am going to find out for myself.'

'Granting that you succeed, sir, how will this benefit the human race?' I asked.

'If the real source of a dream can be discovered, it can be uprooted or at least allayed in its intensity, and dreams and nightmares need no longer terrorize and impair the lives of some sleeping souls. A dream can, and does, kill at times. Again, I have solved how to stop sleep, without seeming injury, and if a continued spell of sleeplessness brings no untoward effects I hope in time to make a sleepless race. The only thing I fear is that my delving into the unknown may bring about my death. There again, Richard, we have the evidence of that something — intuition, premonition, call it what you will. I have a strange feeling that one cannot look into the gulf without being destroyed. Don't ask me why; I can't explain it. On the other hand, it is perhaps only my fancy,' he added in a quiet voice, but his tone did not deceive me.

'You say you have solved how to stop sleep?' I asked.

'Yes; that was not so difficult. Sleep is, of course, brought about by the clogging of the brain with waste and impure products. The real root of the whole trouble is insufficient or used-up oxygen in the blood. This impure blood, on reaching the brain, brings about a deadening effect, and a condition very much akin to a false death is brought about.

'The chemical compound I used to overcome the conditions contains two ingredients. One is the organic compound known as protein, pure protein, if I may use the term, altered and doctored by my own methods so that it makes up for the energy lost during the day's activities and gives a fresh supply of energy to the system. The other ingredient is my own discovery. It is a mineral substance, containing a high percentage of oxygen in a quasi-gaseous form. This, when mixed with protein, produces a blue-looking liquid, and has the power of stopping all desire to sleep, without any consequent loss of mental power or nerve strain, as might be occasioned by a powerful drug or stimulant. I have called this stuff 'Veldoris'.

'It has an incredible fascination,' he went on reminiscently. 'Like opium or cocaine in its attraction. That's the only trouble. I have will enough to break my love for it — at present, but certainly something will have to the done to lessen its incredible potency before I offer it to the world. The weak-willed would very soon go under. Richard, you wouldn't think I hadn't slept for a week, would you? You wouldn't think I've been working day and night for that time?'

This came as a surprise to me. He looked as fresh and active as he had always done, and I unhesitatingly told him so.

'So you see, Richard, Veldoris works perfectly. So much for that. My next move is a trifle more complicated. It consists of being asleep — yet awake. I have invented a machine that throws beams of various colours and merges them into one another by a slowly rotating disk of different-coloured glasses — a kind of vastly improved lime-light.

'Now colours, as you know, under certain conditions, can produce various mental effects, if you allow your will to be governed by them. An insidious green will make you feel sick in time; a restful, hazy heliotrope will make you feel contented and drowsy; a glaring red will keep you wide awake and turn you feverish — and so on. But a combination of all the colours of the spectrum, so to speak, will produce hypnosis — self-hypnosis — if you gaze into the combination long enough. Just the same as sound rhythm can kill you or raise you to heights of sheer, ungovernable ecstasy.

'In sound — although this has nothing to do with my apparatus — your heart unconsciously keeps time with rhythm. If you allowed yourself to be so governed, an organ striking a very deep note — and gradually becoming slower and slower — could kill you. Your heart would stop.

Hence the slowness of a funeral march — the ancients knew a thing or two, Richard! Hence also the gay swiftness of a dance band, that keeps your heart beating fast and makes you feel exhilarated. But I wander from my subject.

'Concentrated gazing into the swirling mass of colours I have devised produces in time a waking sleep. To all intents and purposes the will ceases to be centralized in the brain; no longer does it control the limbs. What happens is that the body does go to sleep, and the controlling brain also, but that something in the mind, the subconscious, or whatever you care to call it, keeps awake, partly by the action of Veldoris, and partly by the colour effects.

'Hence a dream becomes a waking reality, controlled entirely by the subconscious, brought from the normal hazy indefinability into sheer, concrete fact. Just like the somnambulist who walks along a cliff edge, yet whose controlling subconscious mind is fixed upon something in his dream — something light years away from his mundane position — which makes him quite unable to recognize his deadly danger. Hence, as the fear of his danger is removed, so is the danger itself no longer imminent to him. He comes back safely.

'Have you ever thought, Richard, how few sleepwalkers meet their deaths? Well, tonight I am going to explore a dream. If I succeed I shall return and try again and again until I have gathered enough information on the subject to find a way of ridding humanity of the plague of nightmares and so on. I shall communicate with you again in a week's time. If you do not hear anything from me by then, Richard, come and look for me of your own accord. Here is the key to the front door, in case Walmsley should not be in or anything similar happens.'

He handed the key to me very solemnly. I was accustomed to his short dismissals and matter-of-fact way of ending a subject.

I left him shortly after that, much puzzled, and also worried lest I should lose him, for I loved him as a friend and counsellor.

* * *

Six days of the specified week passed by, and I heard nothing from him. Then on the sixth night I had a dream, a dream of such astounding vividness, so clear, so lifelike, that I woke up with a violent start, shaking in every limb. Distinctly I had seen Dr. Veldor, strangely changed somehow, gesticulating and waving his arms at me from some faintly lighted darkness. I heard his voice — but that also was unaccountably different from his normal tones, as also was his manner. He was reviling me, cursing me, screaming threats and abuses upon me. So awful was the force of his rage and anger, so menacing did he appear as he suddenly seemed to come toward me, I awoke.

I did not need anything to tell me that something was wrong. I threw on my clothes and tore downstairs into the hall of the house where I lodged. I had a questioning shout from my landlady and a dim vision of her — a round face topped with a nightcap peering round her door jamb — then I was out in the cold air of the London night. At full speed I streaked down the high roads, through alleyways and back streets, until at last, utterly breathless, I reached the doctor's home.

In another moment I had opened the door and passed into his study. The light was full on, and an open diary lay upon his desk with a smear of ink across it. Beyond, on the far side, another door was slightly ajar, with light streaming from it. I went toward it at a run and flung it open.

I recognized the place at once as the doctor's laboratory. Walmsley, a vaguely comical figure in his long dressing gown, came toward me with a hopeless look on his round face.

'Thank God you've come, sir!' he breathed, clutching my sleeve. 'I haven't known what to do for the good doctor these last few days. He hasn't been normal, sir. He's looked at me with burning eyes and muttered things about 'Veldoris' and suchlike. Just now I heard him shout, and I came downstairs right away, to find him like that, sir. He's — he's dead!' The servant's voice broke huskily.

'Dead!' I exclaimed sharply and strode forward.

I found the doctor sprawled at full-length on a long bench, with a single small pillow. One arm was dangling over the side, and on the floor beneath his limp hand was a blue bottle with the one word 'Veldoris' written across it. It required no expert to realize that he was quite dead, and his death had evidently been a struggle, for his face was set in the most horrified, distorted expression I have ever seen. Above him was his beam instrument, extinguished.

I stood there in silence for a space, hardly knowing what to say or do. There were formalities to be gone through, of course. Then I found a letter, addressed to me propped against a chemical bottle. It contained a lot of things dear to me, which I do not wish to reproduce, but the gist of it was that he absolved everybody from blame in connection with his death, and I would find the full story in his diary.

And that is all I have to tell for my own part. The remainder is Dr. Veldor's own story, pieced from incoherencies in places, but mainly consistent. I give it to the world as coming from the hand of a man who met his death trying to devise a means of ending the terrors of sleep, who tried to probe a little too far into the unknowable — the words of Dr. Veldor, who has since become known in the scientific world as 'the man who never slept'.

★   ★   ★

NOVEMBER 18TH. I kept my word to Richard and set to work the same night to explore the unknown region beyond the living world. I am writing this two days after. I was fully aware as I set my beam machine to work of the dangerous nature of the phenomenon with which I was tampering, but dangerous or otherwise nothing could be learned without trying. So, as on a previous occasion, I took a full dose of the overpowering, insidious Veldoris and lay on the table directly beneath those swirling lights.

I am a man of pretty strong will, and I

succeeded in eventually dissociating myself from bodily trammels. In some strange, indefinable way I knew I was no longer normally awake. My body was like lead. I could not fully comprehend what I was doing; yet I saw quite clearly that iridescent mist of hypnotic colours about me. In a manner, I suppose I was assimilated to a spiritualistic medium.

Then suddenly it seemed to me as though the beam machine had gone out. I was no longer lying flat on my back; instead I was standing in some place that seemed vaguely familiar. A little back street, dimly lighted by lamps, and at the end of it a shining grey expanse that I knew was the Thames River. I looked down at myself. I was in ragged clothing, and shivering with cold.

Quite suddenly I knew where I was. Almost twenty years ago I had stood in the same spot — a ragged, unwanted youth. It was when I had been turned out by my father and had been left to fight my own way in the world. But how in the name of wonder had I returned to this past point in time? While in my dream condition I could not understand, in any instance, how I reached the places I did,

How crystal-clear everything was! None of the vagueness of a dream! I took a step forward to investigate, then somewhere a window slammed through the night. I returned to the mundane beneath my lights and sat up, still shivering. A close inspection of the laboratory revealed that the heater was not functioning properly and that the temperature was very low.

Further, close to where I had been lying on the table, a test tube had slipped out of its rack onto the bench close to my ear. The resultant noise must have been slight, but loud enough to supply the sound of the slamming window.

So, then, at my first effort I had discovered that dreams took one back into a past time to an event of outstanding mental clearness, and that most of the occurrences fitted in by some unexplained freak with occurrences in the present.

I remembered, when I came to ponder, that at that point twenty years ago, a window had slammed, and I had been cold. Funny, then, that a falling test tube and a faulty radiator should produce the coinciding external results twenty years later. I thought of 'mechanized' and 'induced' dreams, and decided that the brain after all is responsive during dreams to external things. *(Or so Dr. Veldor believed at this period. R. F.)*

But that coincidence of events, and my travel backward in time, deeply impressed me. I decided to probe further.

NOVEMBER 19TH. I thought when I discovered Veldoris that I had done mankind a service — that I would be able to pass on to mankind a panacea for all the ills of sleep, and make mankind a thriving and industrious race. Now I have decided otherwise. It is not such joy after all to be deprived of sleep — never for a moment to feel relaxation, never to desire to slumber. This accursed Veldoris! It is deadly in its attraction.

I have tried to overcome its temptation, but it is too strong for me. I cannot do without it. I want sleep, and I want Veldoris. I cannot have both, so I take the latter. I have just returned from a walk about London — a sleeping city. Almost everybody asleep save me. Everybody on earth can sleep save me! I have a growing horror of this wakefulness. I have decided to postpone my next effort until tomorrow night.

NOVEMBER 20TH. After my usual process of self-hypnosis I ultimately found myself standing on a bare and windy plain, with a grey sky that had a flush akin to twilight above me. There was no moon, no stars. I looked down at myself but failed to recognize my form. It was a peculiarly squat affair, with very short, amazingly thick legs, round powerful body, and tremendous hands and arms. An investigative fingering of my face revealed a growth of thick hair. Where was I? What was I? I did not know. The present situation did not seem to fit in with anything I remembered. Even my body was different, and as before I could not, while undergoing the experience, remember anything outside it.

I went forward a few paces, then a remarkable thing happened. I found myself viewing two places simultaneously. Superimposed upon the barren, cheerless plain was Piccadilly Circus. It was daylight, and the seething flood of traffic was at its height. I stood looking upon it all, like an uncomprehending animal — stood looking at the plain, and London. I felt suspended between heaven and earth. Buses and people passed through me, yet I did not feel anything. What had taken place this time? I still had that repulsive body.

There was only one explanation. I was in the fourth dimension — or some dimension or other.

(Be it understood that Dr. Veldor wrote his notes after his return, in the light of normal intelligence. In his form as a brute man he could neither have understood London nor a fourth dimension. R. F.)

By some unexplained paradox of time and space it was night where I was standing, yet daylight in the normal world. Imagine my amazement, when upon a hoarding, I saw a placard, which read: 'Three More Days To See The Cattle Exhibition', and gave the date when the exhibition ended. Although I did not comprehend it then — although I could not even read then and have only my latent memory to describe it by — I know now that I was viewing a time ten years ahead of the present, and Heaven alone knows how many years in advance of the time when I stood on the barren plain . . .

So the dream state did not necessarily take one into the past. Here was a future occurrence; which by some complexity of time relation to the mundane world I was permitted to view.

Then suddenly, out of the grey darkness of the mysterious plain on which I stood, there swept a black, shapeless thing that bore down upon me like an express train. I tried to move, but somehow felt powerless. My limbs refused to act. A blank and freezing terror was in my vitals. It did not hit me; it *absorbed* me!

I have a remembrance of struggling with a sudden return of muscular movement, of grappling desperately with that shapeless, abominable creation of an unknown dimension, of feeling it expand and contract beneath my clutch. Then I fell off the experimental table in my laboratory, to find the lights still above me. I was perspiring freely, and my heart was beating furiously from the recollection of that frightful thing.

Again I have traced certain fundamental truths in my experiences. The creature I had struggled with was one of those awful things that occasionally come into a normal nightmare. The dreaded, impalpable something that expands and contracts and suffocates, until one awakes in a sweating, paralyzed terror. I have proved this seeming figment of imagination to be real! It does exist, in a dimension that I, too, had occupied at some point in my existence — at a point, which, perhaps all of us have at one time inhabited.

I have lived, as a squat, peculiar man of little brain, with all the fears of a primitive man or ape. Long have I known that the 'falling dream' is merely a recollection, from apelike days, handed down, when one fell from a tree to destruction — the stark memory of which still lies in our innermost selves to startle us out of sleep. But I have discovered something new! More and more do I realize that dreams are not imaginative creations, but actual occurrences impressed upon the mind, handed down through the process of evolution, by procreation and heredity, across the gulf of endless time from body to body. It is a sober thought.

As to the superimposition of a future time in London, I can only explain it as being an 'overlap' of the three-dimensional world, related by some paradox of higher mathematics in that moment of unknown past when I was in another dimension and inconceivably far back in the scale of evolution. One fact has become very manifest to me: It is that dream experiences cannot be governed to any particular point. Another point is that time, in the subconscious state, is merely a myth. It is haphazard and indeterminable.

NOVEMBER 21ST. I have made a remarkable discovery. Today I have been working out my data on this subject, and I have discovered why it is that external conditions affect and coincide with subconscious dream states. There is a realm of what I will call force that exists between the conscious and subconscious states. Always, at the time of a dream, that dream occurs in relation to that force, which is related not indirectly to time, which latter cannot be altered. Everything, according to the laws of this force, duplicates itself in some form or other and links the mentality of the dreamer with the occurrences he is dreaming about.

Hence the coinciding moment of the slamming window and the cold. By predetermined calculation this force in relation to time had brought about the seeming coincidence, which really, as I see it now, was mathematical immutability. The process of time had ordained these sounds, as inseparable from the subconscious mind, and nothing could, or ever will, alter it. My experience coinciding with the sounds was also predetermined. More than ever I realize that time is not only as we compute it with our material senses, but it is an endless something that also controls those other and stranger experiences of which I have written. Nothing is done without the dictates of time and force; hence, then, even an 'induced' dream, where sounds are provided to coincide with the sleeper's dreams, is only a dictate of time and force. I appreciate clearly, also, that coincidence is becoming a useless quantity. There is no such thing as coincidence. Perhaps you will ask what force is, then? To which I answer, nobody knows what force *is* — nowhere on earth will you find the explanation of what force is — only what it *does*.

Again, then, I shall venture into this unknown realm. Each time I learn something. My only worry is the increasing demand of this devilish Veldoris. If only it were not so potent, so irresistible!

(Later.) This time I have had an astounding experience, which proves beyond all doubt that dreams are indeed purely the 'leftovers' of some former state of existence or consciousness. Following the hypnotic trance I came to myself in a drawing room of extremely old-fashioned design. Men with long hair and bows upon it were about me. One was chafing my wrists and looking very soulfully into my eyes. The others were solicitous and attentive. An old-fashioned candelabra stood at the chenille-draped mantelshelf. But — *I was a woman!* I had no male conceptions whatever. All my emotions were those of a woman. I knew that I very much loved this dark-eyed youth who was chafing my wrists.

'You fainted, Adeline,' he said in a soft, gentle voice. 'Do you feel better? You must take care with that weak heart of yours, you know.'

I got to my feet unsteadily and looked down at the neat, buckled shoe on my small foot. Again, I say, 1 had no conception then of being anything different from Adeline Laysen, a very-much-sought-after young beauty of the Victorian era. I had no conception of my own self — or at least the self of my own time. Actually, I was living then in what *was* myself.

I spent an evening playing the piano in that very old-fashioned drawing room, then I complained once again of feeling unwell. The lights, the candles, were swirling round. Somebody caught at me as I fell, and I have a distinct remembrance of hearing somebody shout: 'Good Heavens, Marnot, she's dead!'

So I came back again. Try as I would I could not connect the haphazard events that occurred. But then, if that force of which I have written had predetermined everything, the events would occur in relation to the order of the force, not time. I might have the later events before the earlier ones — it all depended on the force relationship to my consciousness.

Looking back over my notes I have found a case where a woman has dreamed of being a drunken man, several times running, yet has never known such a person in real life, and has no idea what it is to be intoxicated. Sufficient evidence surely that I am right in my opinion that dreams are but phases of life from other lives. Sometimes sweet and lovely; at others terrible and bizarre.

I do not feel too happy tonight. Somehow I have a feeling that I am dabbling in things too deep for me — that I am violating some almighty law, which will sooner or later rise up and destroy me. Veldoris is still maintaining its grip upon me, but, strangely enough, I find now that I cannot sleep even when I make effort of will enough to keep away from Veldoris for a space. What is the matter with me? I have just looked in the mirror and I see that my face is old and weary. There are deep furrows round my mouth. It is the face of a drug addict.

NOVEMBER 22ND. If I could only sleep! I am indeed paying the penalty for my fool curiosity. Either with Veldoris or without it, I cannot sleep, so I may as well have Veldoris and spare myself the effort of will power to keep away from it.

(Here was a gap, presumably of some hours, for the writing is resumed in a less steady hand. R. F.)

I cannot understand what has happened to me! Just now I went off into a hypnotic trance without Veldoris! The stuff is mastering me! I never know now when I shall be overcome. It happens without coloured lights — without Veldoris — without any exertion on my part. I am becoming perpetually suspended between two worlds — between that mystery subconscious region and the mundane. Poor Walmsley! I think he is rather frightened of me — and well he might be! I am frightened of myself!

My dream experience this time was not pleasant. I merged into a world of utter blackness — black, that is, from a human standpoint. Yet I seemed to be possessed of some curious optical faculty. I *saw* heat and infra-red rays, and looked through rubber windows as though they were of glass. I read strange wording by the glow of a red-hot iron, and everything about me seemed as bright as day.

What strange dimension had I got into this time? Obviously a dimension where the eyesight was different to ours, where one could see heat and look through a solid. And through it all there lingered, somewhere forgotten yet most desired, a desire for sleep! If only I could sleep! My Heaven, why did I ever try such a fool experiment? Why did I ever attempt to delve into the unknown?

I vanished abruptly from my world of heat into a dimension of utter incredibility. A world where oblongs and cubes mounted end on end and subdivided into long, incomprehensible shapes vanishing in an inky sky, in which were set strange and brilliant stars. I have no idea what dimension or world it was. It faded almost instantly, and I awoke where I am now — sitting at my desk with my diary before me. I am becoming alarmed, yet some unknown power impels me on.

NOVEMBER 23RD. I have not long to live — not long to write down these words. Three times today I have fallen into that hypnotic state between worlds. Veldoris is all I crave; it has become my soul — my being. Yet I crave sleep still more. I must rest! My brain feels as though it will burst, so constant is the strain and stress being placed upon it. It is more than flesh and blood can stand.

I hope I am not a coward — but this is too much. You will find me dead Richard, and, I hope, asleep in the gulf beyond. You will find a bottle near me which will have 'Veldoris' written upon it. You will find the formula for Veldoris in my safe. Pledge me your solemn oath that you will destroy that formula the first thing you do. Try to stop vivid dreams by the aid of what few notes I have given you, but never try to stop sleep. Nature never intended that life should go on perpetually without a rest.

Tonight I have again dropped into that dream world and have had a deadly experience. I have seen a world of flame. I have been forced toward a canyon of flame by barbs with my hands tied behind me. I had a recognizable human form. But, Richard, you were the one who sent me to my doom — or I thought you did. I have seen you upon a throne of some strange, glittering metal, watching my progress toward a furnace, a cleft of flame and death. And you watched with a merciless smile on your face.

Even in that consciousness your name was Richard. I shouted your name with all my power. I reviled you, knowing you for what you are in my normal life — my dearest young friend.

I fell into that gulf of fire; perhaps I died and was reborn into another state of consciousness. I do not know. I remember only that I fell through the floor of the gulf of fire into a world that had no opacity, where I could see through the ground and where no solid seemed to block my body or vision. I got to my feet and walked forward steadily, until presently I came to a solid world again — found myself wandering in drear, unknown streets, a place which I now realise was London. Some strange force compelled me *through* a closed door, and I came to a figure lying asleep in bed.

In an instant I recognized you, not as I really know you, but as Richard the man who had condemned me to the flames. I became seized with a mad fury; I tried to strangle you, but my hands went through you. As I could not do you any physical injury I stood glaring down my hate upon you. I saw you writhe in your sleep. I cursed you for condemning me to the flames. Then suddenly you awoke.

At that instant something seemed to snap within me, and I found myself slowly recovering here before my desk — not refreshed, but more weary and hopeless than ever. I have written down these words; I feel somehow that you will come and find me. Don't think too hard of me, Richard. I have tried — and failed.

You have my record — and you will

also find a letter, which I wrote some days ago, in anticipation of this event.

Now I shall go into the laboratory and lie on that infernal table for the last time, for perhaps I shall now be able to sleep.

Sleep!

5

Mark Grayson Unlimited

As the closest friend of the late Dr. Mark Grayson, I feel that I am called upon to relate the full details of his amazing experiment. I cannot stand idly by and hear him referred to as a lunatic who finally made a mysterious exit from his prison cell, because I knew him to be one of the most brilliant, though maybe misguided, scientists of our time.

From early college days when we had used to room together he had always been interested in interatomic physics, with particular leanings towards Schrodinger, and Heisenberg with his Principle of Indeterminacy. What exactly he gleaned from the treatises and theories of these two great scientific thinkers I did not discover until later years — and then I did it with a vengeance!

After college was over our ways

perforce parted and I heard nothing of Mark for many years. I married, settled down to quite a thriving practice as attorney in New York. Then one day I found that he was in the news — and none too pleasantly either. Apparently he had been ridiculed by the Association of Science for setting forth some new theory connected with the electron. In the report I read of the meeting it was pretty clear that Mark had had the worst of it and as a gesture of protest had resigned his position as Professor of Interatomic Physics to the Association.

Just about like old Mark! Ridicule was the one thing he had never been able to stand, and evidently he had not altered his views much in the passing years. Hearing about him, though, brought old memories back to me and so I wrote him a letter, asking the newspaper to forward it to him. I made a point of sympathizing with him but I also admitted that owing to my limited scientific knowledge I had no idea whether he had been right or wrong. Back came his answer very shortly — his address showed he was living now on Long Island — and it was typical of him:

My dear Arthur —

It was a delight to hear from you again, and even better to have your sympathy. I do not need it, though. It should be given to those dolts in the Association. I verily believe they do not know the difference between an electron and a piece of cheese! Why don't you come over to my place for a few days and renew the friendship? Maybe I can explain to you how monumental a thing it is to be able to detect an electron for the first time in scientific history.

Always yours sincerely,
Mark Grayson.

When I showed the wife the letter she decided to pay a visit to her sister, and it being a fairly quiet period in the city I took time out and went over to Long Island to see what exactly Mark was getting at.

Obviously he had made plenty of

money, anyhow. His home was a truly beautiful place, and adequately staffed by a very immobile manservant and an even more immobile housekeeper. I found later that they were husband and wife, and deaf-mutes. Evidently Mark was taking no chances on his secrets travelling elsewhere. Mark himself was well enough. He was three years my senior, but work and worry had made him look a good deal more than that. His wild, disorderly hair was streaked prematurely with grey, his small, energetic form was even thinner than when he had been a youth — but there was no doubt that the creative fires of energy still burned within him. He moved and talked swiftly. His quick blue eyes darted inquiry and challenge alternately. He was what the novelists would call a restless, highly intellectual soul, with no time for trifles and even less for derision.

I arrived in mid-afternoon and until eight in the evening we exchanged notes of the passed years and recalled the happy things we had done. No word about science escaped his lips. He had remained

194

a bachelor, I think, because his work had kept him too preoccupied to admit of him even looking at a woman, let alone marrying one.

Then, suddenly, without any inducement on my part, he came to the matter I was wondering about. It was after dinner, when he sat chewing a short cigar.

'What do you know about the electron, Arthur?' he asked me, standing with his back to the library fire. 'You are an attorney and an intelligent man. I ask you because I don't want to waste time explaining something you may know already.'

'Always in a hurry, aren't you?' I smiled. 'Well, all I know about an electron is that it is — I think — the smallest particle of electricity.'

'The deplorable uselessness of education!' he groaned, raising his hands deprecatingly. 'Obviously I shall have to start from the beginning if you are ever to understand what I am getting at. Just come along with me, Arthur, and I'll open your eyes.'

Rather amused at his general air of

impatience, I followed him out of the room to his private laboratory, and then stood for a moment or two looking round on instruments and apparatus I could never hope to understand. He perched himself on a stool, and now he was amidst these weird creations of his genius he looked really at home.

'An electron has so far only been a theory — or better still a probability,' he said, his eyes fixed on me.

I squatted down on an empty crate opposite him.

'One of the big stumbling blocks to scientific progress has been the inability of man to say that the electron is either here or there,' he went on. 'Until I studied the problem we knew that the electron, while obeying the mathematical laws of waves and ripples, was also a particle. But it could not be placed. It existed somewhere within a wave group, but that wave group was indefinite in extent. It had no sharp limitation. It just trailed off into surrounding space, even into other dimensions. For all we knew it might extend into infinity. So far all we have known is that the electron exists, but that its exact position is purely a probability in the equation of waves.'

'You're going pretty deep, Mark,' I said, pondering. 'But go on — I'll try and follow you.'

'You recall that I used to study Heinsberg a lot? He outlined the Principle of Indeterminacy — that it is impossible to know both the position and velocity of an electron at a chosen moment. Measure one and the other changes immediately. Since both factors are necessary to an absolute deduction it looked as if Man would never be able to metaphorically put his finger on the electron's position. Of course, approximate deductions could be made by the very reason of the electron's area of waves being so inconceivably small. But science does not like things to approximate, Arthur. It demands incontestable fact.'

Mark paused for a moment, drawing at his cigar. Then he gave a rather cynical grin.

'I found out how to extend the area of an electron wave,' he commented. 'Instead of allowing the waves to be infinitesimal and shading off into space or other dimensions, I devised electrical equipment reacting directly on the subatomic waves of matter. The result is that I can extend the wave area of an electron indefinitely, and more than that! The strain produced by extending these waves produces a definite reaction in one exact part of the extended wave. In that exact part we find — the electron! I believe, had I decided to finish the subatomic microscope I had in mind, it would have been possible to view the electron as one would a planet through a telescope. But I am not going on with that idea — not now.'

A hard note had crept into his voice — and I glanced at him in surprise.

'But why not?' I exclaimed. 'It would surely be the greatest achievement of your career?'

'You remember how I was treated by the Association?' he asked bitterly. 'Their attitude is why I have called an end to my experiment. The Association was of the opinion that my discovery was absurd — that years of experiment had served to turn my head! Far from them agreeing to look into my findings, or perhaps helping me to finish off the finer details of the discovery, they laughed me to scorn. Prejudice still exists, Arthur, even in these days. For that very reason I am going to have my revenge on them — on everybody on this whole stupid planet! You can't laugh at science and get away with it.'

The change in his manner rather startled me for a moment. I had always known him to be a pretty erratic sort of fellow, with perhaps a good share of that curious vindictiveness that sometimes goes alongside great genius, but here something ugly was cropping up. It was in every line of his bearing.

'What more details could be needed to such an experiment?' I asked quietly, trying to keep him on the straight track.

'Plenty! You see, I was handicapped at the Association because I was not able to give a concrete demonstration of my theory. To have done that would have produced unpredictable results. You see, Arthur, this extension of electronic wavelength automatically crushes — or at least telescopes — the wavelengths of the electrons immediately surrounding them, and the effect would be progressive. It would be rather like a railway siding. You have seen how a truck is shunted, and how perhaps a hundred trucks all jolt after the first one has been shoved by the locomotive? That is the same effect in principle.

'To extend one area will mean a progressive jolting of electronic waves in all directions from the source of the disturbance. Now, an electron wave has a range that may pass into infinity — which means, into the greater macrocosm of our universe. It also operates, as Schrodinger told us, in three dimensions. But two electrons operate in six dimensions, three in nine, and so forth, Can you for a moment grasp the bewildering complexity of one electron with its wavelength held out in indefinite stress for maximum distance? An area would be disturbed all around it and the very structure of space and matter would be shifted!'

'In that case,' I said, looking at him

fixedly and thinking hard, 'it might mean the end of the world!'

'It would,' he said, grinning. 'Or at least it would, if I know my scientific facts. What's needed is careful experiment to render such a possibility impossible. I have not enlarged an electron wave yet, but I know I could do it. It might take me many years to find a way of isolating this freak wave to prevent a wholesale disturbance, but for this the Association is not prepared to wait. They wanted results immediately. Because I had to refrain from giving them, I — well, I walked out.'

'Then you are going to complete the problem on your own?' I asked.

He stubbed out his cigar, and got off the stool. Coming over to me he regarded me steadily.

'No. I am not!' His voice was deadly quiet. 'I realise that if science in this day and age cannot credit the word of one of its most famous members, it is time that such science and the devotees of it be destroyed! I am going to extend the area of an electron wave and consequences be hanged!'

I got up quickly and caught at his arm.

'But you just said it would be dangerous!' I protested.

'That it would, perhaps, destroy the world?' he went on. 'Yes that's exactly what I believe it will do. But don't you see, it will have proved that I am right. I'll have proved I can extend the wave of an electron. If it does not destroy the world it will mean that the area is there ready to view once a subatomic microscope is prepared. I shall have provided the proof. If it does destroy the world — well, I'd sooner lose a mighty discovery and my own life in a cataclysm than have a lot of fools grinning at me!'

'Look here, Mark, you can't do this!' I said firmly, holding on to him. 'You are only looking at it from your own viewpoint. You are bitter and vindictive, like you used to be at school when old Haldane said you dreamed too much. I steered you right then, and I'm going to now. You can't do this thing!'

Mark stared at me a moment. His face hardened, became ruthless.

'I can — and I'm going to,' he

answered steadily. 'I asked you to come here so that you can be a witness to my actions. I shall need proof if my experiment is successful and the world still stays in place afterwards . . . I'm not mad, you know,' he added seriously.

No, he was not mad — not in the accepted sense, anyway. But he was consumed with mortified rage that anybody should dare to question his genius. Amazing though it was, it seemed I had on my hands the unenviable job of trying to save a whole universe from his too clever hands.

I released him and stood trying to think things out, my mind running round the idea of physical violence. He left me and walked across to a complicated switchboard controlling many massive and unfamiliar instruments.

'This is my electron-wave extender,' he said. 'It reacts on the subatomic waves. The energy it generates strikes into the densest part of the electron waves. By this means they do not shade off into infinity but are built up in intensity until they have the same strength as the source.

Since electrons are everywhere, be it matter or space, it simply does not signify where I apply the energy. But for the sake of accuracy it might as well be a fixed point.'

He turned aside and picked up a small sealed ampoule. It looked to be empty. Gently he set it down on the big circular plate immediately within the range of his queerly fashioned projectors.

'This ampoule is filled with hydrogen gas,' he explained. If you remember your physics you will recall that it is the least dense substance in our material Periodic Table, and therefore the easiest one to deal with in the search for an electron — granting there ever is a search later on.'

He began to fiddle with switches and controls, and all of a sudden it occurred to me what he was planning to do while I simply stood and watched. I acted instantly! Lunging at him, I caught his arm just as he threw the master switch. He staggered backwards and fell, half sprawling, across the flat metal plate where he had laid his ampoule of hydrogen. For a second or two he just lay there, dazed, then I hauled him up again, pushed him into a chair and snapped off the master switch I had seen him operate.

'You are not going to do this thing,' I declared grimly. 'Not even if I have to beat the daylights out of you to make you see reason. Later on you'll thank me, too.'

He sat there looking at me, glowering in fact — then gradually the light died out of his eyes and he got to his feet.

'I wonder if you realize something?' he said slowly. 'I fell on that plate right in the area of that energy of mine! It hit me — all over! What I had intended for the hydrogen-sample reacted on me instead. I wonder what will happen?' he finished, pondering.

'Nothing,' I assured him. 'You weren't under the influence long enough for anything to happen.'

He did not say anything for a moment, then he gave a little shrug.

'Just chance that it happened that way,' he shrugged. 'It might prove to be interesting, later on.'

I could plainly see that whatever danger there might be did not distress him in the least. He was true scientist enough to be always interested in the unusual, even if he was the victim.

'Let's get back to the library,' I urged him. 'You need to rest up a bit. Too much work and too much ridicule haven't done you any good, you know.'

He smiled and then nodded, but though he said nothing I could tell that some deep thought or other was at the back of his mind . . .

★ ★ ★

The following day, much to my annoyance, I received an urgent telephone call from home requesting my presence at the office right away for an important legal case — so, just as I had been getting interested I was forced to take my leave of Mark and plunge forthwith into the intricacies of a criminal action.

He parted from me cordially enough, but I noticed an enigmatic smile about his lips as he shook hands. It was the smile of a man who knows something tremendous and won't speak about it. Then, back in

New York, with all the curriculum of legal work around me, I soon forgot all about Mark and his amazing doings.

For a week anyway — then one evening I was working late in my office when I saw somebody standing before me at the desk. For a second or two I questioned the credibility of it because I had locked the door to ensure privacy and the window was thirty-five stories up. Yet there he was — Mark Grayson, smiling cynically, his hair disordered, and his body having a curiously transparent quality.

'Mark!' I exclaimed, astounded, getting up and stretching out my hand in greeting. 'How are you? How did you get in?'

Then, in a flash he was gone! I blinked, rubbed my eyes, then went over to the switch and put the lights on. So far I had only had the desk lamp in action. He had disappeared all right.

I was not exactly frightened, just puzzled. I am not a believer in ghosts, but I do think there is something to premonition and pre-vision. Suppose he had died at the self-same moment and that I had had a pre-death visitation? Immediately I reached for the telephone. His voice answered me promptly enough.

'You saw me?' he repeated, as I explained matters. 'Well, maybe you need your eyes tested. Or else . . . ' He stopped and I guessed he was thinking hard. 'Sort of transparent?' he asked pensively.

'Seemed so — like a fairly solid ghost; I could just see the wall through you — or it, or whatever it was.'

'Mighty interesting, because at the exact time you've mentioned I was thinking about you,' he said. 'I must study this over carefully. It may be the first reaction of that accidental fall I had into the midst of that energy machine of mine.'

'You are feeling well?' I asked anxiously.

'Never better. And I'm not going to destroy the world, so don't you worry. Your commonsense lecture did me good. I mean to find a way to produce electronic isolation. See you again.'

I rang off, sat thinking for a moment or two, then shrugged my shoulders. If there was a scientific explanation for it I certainly did not know what it was . . .

As it transpired, though, this was only the beginning. Two more days went by, then the newspapers published a full column on Mark Grayson. When I read it I found it had been culled from the experiences of quite a lot of different people in widely separated parts of the country. Each person interviewed reported having seen a vaguely transparent figure resembling Mark Grayson. Sometimes he had been observed within five minutes, in places as much as two hundred miles apart. Some witnesses, though perhaps they were drawing on their imaginations, declared that he had merged into two and even three persons, all identical. This had happened while the witnesses were watching him.

To me, especially, it was puzzling, and I wished my legal work over so that I could pay him another visit. The first moment I was free, I hurried to Long Island and found him, apparently not disturbed, though he did not look as well as he had on my earlier trip.

'Glad you've come,' he said, in that offhand way he had, when we were in his laboratory. 'These happenings are rather alarming if you don't understand them. As it happens I do, partly. You know, I've been having the devil of a time with newspaper men. They have been here pestering me. It appears that I am rapidly becoming a public nuisance. All I can do is deny everything, and that does not improve my case very much. If I am not careful I'm likely to find myself in an ugly mess.'

'But how in the world do you account for these appearances of yourself in so many widely differing places?' I demanded. 'You could never have been to such places. Time and distance would not permit it!'

'I think I have unlocked a door of science which I never intended to touch,' he said, thinking. 'And it may mean the end of me. It's likely the extension of how an electronic wavelength reacts differently in a living organism to what it does in inert matter. A piece of iron, for instance, would transmit disturbance to all surrounding matter and bring about a general cataclysm, but organic, or living matter, is different. The effect is transmitted through that body until it is dissipated!

'Mind force enters into it, too. Living matter is at the behest of the mind, as we know, but so far only the living body itself has responded to the mind. In my case it is different. By accidentally falling into the area of that energy transmission I enlarged the wavelength of a whole mass of my electrons indefinitely, displaced the energy thereof, if you will. The result is that confusion has entered into my matter makeup. The displacement of the wavelengths has produced an emission of energy, and each time the energy passes away it has to resolve itself. That is electronic law. The resolution takes the form of a complete image of me, a thin, attenuated image, which travels immediately to the spot I happen to be thinking of at the time, or somewhere in the immediate vicinity, Mind is at the back of it all the time because mind is at the back of the parent body.

'But there is a price for it, Arthur. With each emission of energy, as more electrons extend their wavelengths and pass away from my physical makeup, I lose substance and weight. Mind I cannot lose, because that is an eternal quality.'

I was bewildered by what he had told me. 'I don't half grasp all this,' I said. 'Where is it going to end?'

'I don't know,' he muttered. 'I believe it has only just begun. A series of thinly spaced electron setups part from me at intervals and become ghosts of Mark Grayson. There are tens of thousands of Mark Graysons remaining in my make up yet. As I told you, one electron takes three dimensions; two, six; three, nine — and so on progressively. In time I imagine that my images will not only be hurtling to different parts of the Earth but into other spaces, dimensions, times, and worlds. In other words I am being radiated into infinity and multiple-infinity. Maybe it is a just judgment for the plan I had to destroy the world and perhaps the universe.'

'But for me it would never have happened,' I protested. 'I pushed you onto that plate!'

'And by so doing you perhaps saved the world.' He shrugged. 'What's the difference? It happened, and I'm prepared to abide by it.'

That was how the matter stood with him. There was not much I could do about it, anyway, not being a particularly good scientist. But the interest of this amazing phenomenon had gripped me so hard that I sent over a call to the wife and told her I was stopping with Grayson for a day or two as he was not very well. By this decision I entered into the most astonishing few days any man ever lived.

At intervals — intervals which increased in frequency as time passed — I actually saw this parting of electronic energy from Mark Grayson. It was rather like one of those trick shots in a movie where a dreamer gets out of himself and walks about.

Suddenly, even while talking to me, or having a meal, or seated in a chair, an image of Mark would flash out from him in a hazy glow, go right through wall, floor, or ceiling and vanish. All he did was smile wryly, recall exactly what he had been thinking about at that moment, and sure enough the image was later reported to have been seen in that exact spot.

At first this used to happen at intervals of three hours. Then as the weird progressive change built up within him, as the energy he had absorbed extended more and more multi-thousands of electron wavelengths inside him, it happened more repeatedly, until in two more days as many as twelve images parted from him in thirty minutes. In some cases they were in triplicate. I completely lost count of how many Mark Graysons went out, but we learned plenty from the television, radio and newspapers. Some of the reports were pathetic, some startling, and others downright ludicrous.

In a far Western state a woman dying of cancer had been praying for a vision to restore her. At that identical time some quirk of Grayson's mind had sent an image right into her bedroom, a place he had merely envisaged in thought. The woman had seen the vision and been instantly cured.

In another case a famous banker had demanded action by the police because Mark had appeared through the closed doors of a secret conference and heard all the details of a great international finance deal. In yet another instance an image had appeared in England where a high-pressure estate agent had been trying to sell a castle to a wealthy traveller. The traveller had refused to buy because there was no sign of the reputed ghost. A Mark Grayson transparency glimpsed in the aged cloisters had made that agent a richer man.

Silly, trivial things, but they give an idea of what distances the parting electrons of Mark Grayson travelled, distances no longer trammelled to the ordinary limits of an electron wavelength. Then, always the true scientist, he began to see that undisciplined journeying by his images are useless. He might as well do something with them. For, as he told me, he knew what they saw and felt by reason of the mind reaction they carried. Because of this, he gradually became less sure of himself. As the images increased to the multiples he inevitably received multiple impressions, was in some cases aware of being in half a dozen places at once.

But he was determined to make something of his doom, for that was inevitably what was coming, As he got to the place where the images were so numerous they were not confined to three dimensions but to six, nine, twelve, and multiples of three for every electron, he went literally a-roaming, and each time he told me what he had seen and done. I can only report this as he explained it.

He passed into the sixth dimension and found it populated as freely as our own three, but by beings who were purely mathematical because of their environment. He wandered across the red sands of Mars and found a truly dead world, walked beneath the clouds of torrid Venus, wandered across sun-scorched Mercury. He had in fact the supreme chance of all creation, the ability to roam as an actual thought-projected image into all the places locked so far to science.

He told me of his journeys through the hottest suns, of his visits to the centres of blazing Sirius and Antares. Then some whim changed his course. He had all Time open to him, too, as more and more electrons swept him into the multiple dimensions demanded of them.

He walked in the Cretaceous and Carboniferous Periods, saw the beginning and end of the world, established facts of history, which I wrote down and stated vital facts of the future, which only the passage of time can prove to lesser mortals. He saw ahead of us not peace and content but a world of struggle and dreadful turmoil until Man should really come to understand that all life, intelligence, power, and conception are mental and not physical.

Plainly, Mark Grayson, unlimited in number of images and unlimited by any mortal or material barrier, was for three brief weeks a god. Then he tired of his wanderings and the vast things he had learned. The terrific strain on his mental and physical makeup broke him down. Unutterably weary, for his bodily energy had decreased with every set of electrons to pass from it, he finally ceased his mental roaming and let the images go whither chance willed. In consequence they appeared here, there, and everywhere without direction. Sometimes in the city, sometimes in the country, sometimes for good, sometimes for ill — until the very complexity of his appearances and the secrets he supposedly learned caused big shots to add their complaints to that of banker Joseph Runthorne and finally the police came to investigate. I was present when they arrived. I tried in vain to convince them that my friend was ill and could not be disturbed.

He was sitting in the laboratory when they arrested him — a pale, white-haired man now, lines of weariness traced on his face.

'Do you deny, Dr. Grayson, that you have been projecting images of yourself here, there, and about?' asked the officer in charge. 'Do you assert you haven't been using these images for the learning of secrets and the — er — violation of personal privacy?'

Grayson smiled wanly. 'I admit the first and deny the second. Not that it matters. I have seen the beginning and end of the world, the beginning and end of space.'

It was a pity he said this for it sounded

crazy. It was on this ground that he was brought up for trial. I was present too, of course, as chief witness and I employed a brother lawyer of outstanding skill to defend him. But unfortunately Mark prejudiced his chances by his technical explanations.

To me, knowing him as he had been, it was quite clear that the mass of knowledge he had amassed and the energy he was still losing had caused him to lose his grip on his mind. He sounded — and maybe he was — crazy. Certainly the regular glowing of light about him which pronounced the departure of more images did a great deal to get him convicted as a criminal lunatic. He was removed to prison to await confinement in an institution for the criminally insane.

I was allowed to see him for a few minutes, and found him quite rational again. I took good care to keep my distance in the cell though, for now the glow was almost continuing. He looked as if he were painted to phosphorescence.

'I've not far to go, Arthur,' he said soberly, as I sat looking at him. 'The energy which began in leaps has increased to a positive continuous discharge. Life energy — electronic energy — is flowing out of me like water down a sluice. In a myriad directions, in a myriad dimensions and spaces, images of me must be flashing, appearing, disappearing, shading off into infinite dimensions we cannot even guess at. See — look here!'

He laid his hand on the bunk and for the first time I saw that it was translucent. He was becoming as transparent as glass.

'When the last scrap of energy has exhausted itself, it will be the end of Mark Grayson, and thank God for it!' he said. 'You have been my true friend, so do me a favour. Tell all you know about me to the Science Association. Hand them the notes you have made. They will perhaps believe. Tell them to destroy that machine of mine. Things like this are not for Man to understand until he has learned a lot more science.'

With this I had to leave for my time was up. Then, four days later, I read this in the paper under big headlines:

Mark Grayson Disappears!

Dr. Mark Grayson, the famous scientist, convicted recently as criminally insane and awaiting entry into an asylum, was found today to have vanished from his prison cell, and there is no sign of how the escape was effected. It is presumed that it was accomplished scientifically because there is no trace of window or door having been tampered with. The police are conducting an immediate search.

Needless to say, the police never found him, and they never will. Obviously his last scrap of energy had gone and he is at last untrammelled — or at least his great mind is.

For myself, I put his case before the association and they have promised to examine my notes, of which this is a short history, written to disprove him the lunatic he was thought to be. I say that he was a genius, but before his time. As to whether my act of knocking him on that plate saved the world or not I leave you, and science, to judge.

Not that the last of his images has even now been seen. Electronic radiations still reproduce — or at least rebound — from the subetherial waves of matter, and only last night while out with my wife we both saw a hazy image of Mark for a moment on the other side of the street, which immediately vanished. They have been reported from other parts of the world, too.

Until the last state of unbalance is overcome the world will be forced to remember Mark Grayson, and for my part I want to see that the world shall never forget him.

6

Later Than You Think

Martin Wilson had been repairing clocks for as long as he could remember. He was quite sure he would always be repairing clocks. He did not mind if he died repairing clocks.

His small shop in a street off one of London's busiest thoroughfares was inconspicuous, even medieval. It had windows that belonged to a forgotten time. They bowed out and were small-paned, like something Dickensian. Behind them was a conglomeration of clocks, some going, some not, but all of them valuable for their very antiquity.

Had he wished, Martin Wilson could have netted a small fortune from his collection, but money simply did not interest him. All he wanted was to make and repair clocks, to fondle them, to take them apart and put them together again.

From the busy little ticking of a watch to the stately beating of a lordly grandfather he knew every pulse and throb. The sound of clocks comprised his world, his everything. His customers brought clocks to him for two reasons: some because they were — quite mistakenly — sorry for the grey-haired old man who was apparently too frail to make a living any other way; others because of his superb workmanship.

This September night he was, as usual, busy, and also — as usual — he had forgotten to draw the blinds over the window or lock the door. Outside, it was drizzling gently and the air was stifling warm with a hangover from summer. The few lamps that lighted the narrow street were casting back from the glare of wet flagstones. At the far end of his shop Martin Wilson worked under an electric bulb hanging low from a length of flex, putting the finishing touches to a recalcitrant marble timepiece. He smiled as he wound it and then listened attentively to its steady ticking.

He glanced up at the master-clock on

the opposite wall. The master-clock's big pendulum was swinging deliberately. It was exactly ten. Martin Wilson adjusted the hands of the marble clock and then stood it amongst the half dozen other timepieces he had repaired during the day.

For a moment there was something unexpected. Martin Wilson felt as though he were not looking at clocks but at something dark. It was like a shadow interceding between the clocks and the electric bulb. Their bright, burnished glitter faded and became opaque and meaningless. The clicking and ticking and tocking faded into a jumble of sounds, which became discord . . . Then everything was back as it had been.

Martin Wilson was puzzled. He leaned forward in curiosity, pressing hard against the edge of his workbench. He felt something grind in his pocket but he was too confused for the moment to pay heed.

'Good evening.'

Martin Wilson straightened in surprise. He had not heard the shop door open or shut.

Indeed he had never anticipated a customer at such a late hour. The man was standing at the other side of the bench, a black raincoat turned up about his ears and a dark soft hat pulled well down, so that it was difficult to see his face. Raindrops gleamed like sprinkled diamonds as he moved into the diagonal radiance of the low-hanging lamp.

'Good evening sir,' the old clockmaker wiped his oily hands on a rag and came forward.

'Something I can do for you?'

The stranger seemed to reflect and Martin Wilson fancied he saw a ghostly smile.

'It may sound rather silly,' the stranger said, 'but I'd like to know the *time*. I have no watch, nor have I seen a clock in quite a little while. I'm wondering how late it is.'

'It's just on ten o'clock.'

The old clockmaker stopped; staring at the pendulum clock on the far wall. The pendulum had ceased swinging, for the first time since the clock had been constructed.

'It is later than you think,' the stranger

murmured. He had a low, pleasing voice with a curious alien rhythm in it.

'I don't understand it,' Martin Wilson stared hard at the silent master-clock with its motionless, vertical pendulum.

'That clock has never stopped before . . . '

'Perhaps,' the stranger suggested, 'you might have some other clock by which I may learn the time?'

'Surely!' The old man smiled at the absurdity of the idea. 'Outside of my master-clock, though, there is only one other time piece I trust — my watch.'

He pulled it out of his waistcoat pocket and gazed at it. His frown deepened. The glass had been crushed to powder, blocking the second and minute hands. The watch too had stopped at exactly ten o'clock.

'You *are* unfortunate,' the stranger murmured, leaning forward so that the light made the raindrops scintillate.

'I remember doing this,' Martin Wilson replied, musing. 'I leaned on the bench here. I must have crushed my watch. It was just before you came in . . . I must repair it when I have the chance.' He returned the watch to his pocket and surveyed the busily ticking clocks on the workbench. 'It's seven minutes past ten,' he said finally.

'Thank, you, the stranger said, but he made no effort to go. The old man looked at the master-clock again and sighed.

'You shouldn't have done that, William,' he said seriously.

'William?' the stranger repeated, and Martin Wilson smiled. 'My master-clock, sir. I have names for all my clocks. They are my children. You see, I never married. I have never known the love of a woman or of children of my own. Always it has been clocks.'

The stranger said nothing. The deep silence of the drizzling night was outside and the quiet of the shop was only broken by the pedantic rhythm of a grandfather's pendulum and the busy little ticking of an alarm. In varying degrees of enthusiasm the other clocks were keeping in step. The stranger seemed to listen to them for a while and then stirred slightly.

For a moment the light caught his face and was gone. Martin Wilson did not quite know what to think. He was trying to fathom what it was like to expect to see a face and yet *not* see one. There did not seem to be a face at all, only some kind of indeterminate shadow which, as he unconsciously moved towards it to look more closely, became all the darker.

'You are curious as to my identity, my friend?' the stranger asked, in his mellow, cultured voice. Martin Wilson shrugged.

'I admit I've never seen you before,' he mused.

'I have come a long way, and I am somewhat tired. Would you consider it a liberty if I were to sit down and rest for a while?'

'Please do.'

The stranger turned and pulled forth a chair from his own side of the bench. He settled on it, his back to the light so that his face was thrown into an even deeper shadow than before. A chiming clock struck the quarter hour. It aroused Martin Wilson from a spell of thought. His eyes moved from the glistening drops on the stranger's hat and shoulders to the still silent master-clock.

'Since you wish to rest, sir, and I am in

no hurry, would you mind if I worked?' he asked.

'My dear friend, please do,' the stranger urged. 'Not for a moment do I wish to delay your industry. Men with your touch are so rare.'

'Are they? I'm — I'm sort of glad to hear you say that. I take myself so much for granted — Excuse me, but I must see what is wrong with William.'

Martin Wilson shambled out from behind the bench and searched amongst the lumber of the shop until he had unearthed a pair of steps. He straddled them, climbed up to the penultimate step, then shoved and heaved until he had the wall clock free of its massive nail.

As though the clock were a sleeping child he cradled it in his arm and descended slowly to the floor again, laying the clock face upward on the bench.

'I never knew I had that much strength,' he remarked, surprised. 'This clock is heavy — solid mahogany frame.'

'Sometimes,' the stranger said broodingly, 'we do not realise how strong we really are.'

There was again that glimpse of something where a face should have been and was not.

Martin Wilson wondered if he ought to be frightened by his extraordinary visitor. For some reason he was not. He felt he accepted the occurrence as the most natural thing in the world.

The complexity, the mystery of it, did not trouble him in the least.

Reaching to the tool-rack over the bench he took down a screwdriver and began to detach the clock from its frame. It looked as though the stranger was watching his activities. At last Martin Wilson had the clock free, and detaching the pendulum, he laid the clock face down and gazed at the polished brass works.

'Beautifully intricate,' the stranger commented. 'Obviously constructed by an expert.'

'*I* made it,' the old clockmaker responded. 'Thirty years ago. It was an old Swiss model. I took it to pieces, rebuilt it, and since that time it has never varied more than a few seconds either way. I just don't understand why it should have stopped like this. There doesn't appear to be anything wrong with it.'

He contemplated it, his slender fingers testing the cogs and escapement. Finally he shrugged. With a pair of forceps he unfastened the clamps holding the back in position and lifted it gently. Cogs and pinion-wheels, their supports gone, fell askew. One little spindle rolled forth, a glittering line under the light, and tottered to a standstill.

'You are going to try and repair it?' the stranger inquired.

'If it takes me all night!'

The stranger moved again, ever so slightly, and seemed to be preparing to watch. Martin Wilson glanced towards the door, entirely from force of habit. It still seemed to be drizzling.

Nobody was passing — which was odd. It was as though he and the stranger were the only two people in the universe. So quiet, except for the endless chorus from the clocks.

Shadowy, too, save just in this one spot where the naked glare smote on the clock that would not go.

One by one Martin Wilson took the parts and placed them on the bench, until at last he had the bare frame of the clock and a heap of wheels and spindles. He had forgotten what time it was. For some reason he did not even care. The stranger was still watching absorbedly, and presently he made a comment.

'You know my friend, I have the strangest conviction. I do not think that clock will ever go again.'

'With my workmanship,' Martin Wilson told him, with reasonable pride, 'it cannot fail to.'

'Workmanship, yes, but you are forgetting a deeper issue. What does a clock do? It measures time. It has to work *in* that advancing time in order to register it. Right?'

'I — suppose so,' Martin Wilson agreed, putting a spring into a small receptacle filled with paraffin.

'It *is* so,' the stranger insisted with quiet firmness. 'When you have repaired the clock it will not go, for the simple reason that it can never again catch up on the time it has lost. That time has gone — forever.'

The old man paused in his work and looked troubled. 'How so? If I put the fingers to the correct time and start the pendulum swinging, the clock will go. It cannot fail to.'

'It can fail to, and it will. It stopped at ten. Very well, let us suppose it will be two in the morning before you have assembled it ready for going again. How many hours will have passed during the repairing?'

'Four,' answered Martin Wilson mechanically, removing the saturated spring and wiping it.

'Four hours gone that can never be recalled. To simply adjust the fingers four hours ahead does not mean a thing. You are asking the clock to tell a lie. It has not *lived* through that time, so how can it register it? It is like asking a dead man to come back to life after four hours and carry on as though nothing had happened.'

There was a long silence then Martin Wilson said: 'It will go, I'm convinced of it.'

The stranger said nothing further. He watched the old man's hands at work. The clocks chimed. The hours sped. It surprised Martin Wilson to find that it was striking two when he had the clock reassembled once again. Cradling it in his arms, the pendulum in his free hand, he mounted the steps up to the nail in the wall. Gently he slid the clock back into position and hung the pendulum carefully. With a delicate finger he touched it. It swung to and fro.

'There!' he exclaimed, smiling.

The stranger had risen from his chair and was in the deep shadow cast by the grandfather. It was hardly possible to see him as he gazed upwards. 'It is not going,' he stated quietly.

'It's not — ?' Martin Wilson looked at it and then started.

The stranger had spoken the truth. The initial swinging of the pendulum was slowing down. There was no steady ticking from the escape mechanism.

The old clockmaker opened the front of the clock and peered up into the works. He could see the escapement working perfectly, and yet the clock was not going. Its fingers were still at ten o'clock and the pendulum was slowing — slowing — stopped.

'This is impossible!' the old man declared. 'Am I not a master clock maker? Why should this one defy me?'

'It does not defy you, my friend. It is as I told you: You are trying to make it operate in a time that does not exist.'

'But surely, if I advance it to seven minutes past two, which is the time now, it will then go?'

'No; to get the fingers there you will have to make a record of the intervening hours on the dial, hours which the clock has never truly registered. It cannot do it, anymore than you could reach Tuesday morning by being dead on Saturday, Sunday and Monday.'

'But clocks are things of metal,' Martin Wilson protested. 'They do not think! They cannot reason the passage of hours!'

'My friend, the intervening time has not existed, either for the clock . . . or you.'

The old man blinked and stared down at the shadowy figure. 'Or for me?' he asked.

'I am trying to tell you that Time is not yours to do with as you wish, my friend. Like anybody else you merely borrow it as an intangible medium in which to perform certain acts. To you, to every-body, there comes a moment when the supply of time must run out. It has run out for you — and the clock.'

Martin Wilson descended slowly to the floor. 'These other clocks are going,' he remarked.

'Exactly — because they did not stop. There is no reason why they should not continue to go since they are recording time faithfully. They are living through normal time: you are not.'

The old man scratched the back of his neck. 'Y'know sir, I haven't the vaguest idea what you are talking about. Do you mean to tell me that my master-clock will never go again?'

'Not whilst you and I are here.'

The silence seemed to deepen even more, muting even the ticking of the clocks. Martin Wilson spoke in so low a voice he was hardly audible. 'Who *are* you?' he breathed.

The stranger moved and came slowly into the light.

For the first time Martin Wilson looked

on the face which was not a face but a — He took a sharp step backwards, appalled.

'Don't be alarmed my friend. Now you know the truth. You have not feared me so far. There is no reason why you should do so now.' The stranger paused and then asked quietly, 'Well, shall we go?'

'Yes,' Martin Wilson muttered. 'Yes, we'll go. Now I know what you mean by the clock never going as long as we remain.'

The stranger moved and the old man fell into step beside him. They went across the shop to the front door and it had never seemed so far away. The nearer they went to it, the more it appeared to recede, until it was lost in a vast corridor, almost a tunnel in space, becoming darker and darker in which every sound of the living world was swallowed up.

THE END

CLIMATE INCORPORATED
THE FIVE MATCHBOXES
EXCEPT FOR ONE THING
BLACK MARIA, M.A.
ONE STEP TOO FAR
THE THIRTY-FIRST OF JUNE
THE FROZEN LIMIT
ONE REMAINED SEATED
THE MURDERED SCHOOLGIRL
SECRET OF THE RING
OTHER EYES WATCHING
I SPY . . .
FOOL'S PARADISE
DON'T TOUCH ME
THE FOURTH DOOR
THE SPIKED BOY
THE SLITHERERS
MAN OF TWO WORLDS
THE ATLANTIC TUNNEL
THE EMPTY COFFINS
LIQUID DEATH
PATTERN OF MURDER
NEBULA
THE LIE DESTROYER
PRISONER OF TIME

We do hope that you have enjoyed reading this large print book.

Did you know that all of our titles are available for purchase?

We publish a wide range of high quality large print books including:
Romances, Mysteries, Classics
General Fiction
Non Fiction and Westerns

Special interest titles available in large print are:
The Little Oxford Dictionary
Music Book, Song Book
Hymn Book, Service Book

Also available from us courtesy of Oxford University Press:
Young Readers' Dictionary
(large print edition)
Young Readers' Thesaurus
(large print edition)

For further information or a free brochure, please contact us at:
Ulverscroft Large Print Books Ltd.,
The Green, Bradgate Road, Anstey,
Leicester, LE7 7FU, England.
Tel: (00 44) **0116 236 4325**
Fax: (00 44) **0116 234 0205**